THE GUN-THROWERS

THE
GUN-THROWERS

Steve Frazee

Chivers Press • G.K. Hall & Co.
Bath, England Thorndike, Maine USA

This Large Print edition is published by Chivers Press, England, and by G.K. Hall & Co., USA.

Published in 1999 in the U.K. by arrangement with the author, care of Golden West Literary Agency.

Published in 1999 in the U.S. by arrangement with Golden West Literary Agency.

U.K. Hardcover   ISBN 0-7540-3745-2   (Chivers Large Print)
U.K. Softcover   ISBN 0-7540-3746-0   (Camden Large Print)
U.S. Softcover   ISBN 0-7838-8579-2   (Nightingale Series Edition)

The Gun-Throwers, originally published under the title *One More Hill to Hell* in *Fifteen Western Tales*, copyright, 1950, by Popular Publications, Inc.

Great Medicine, originally published in *Gunsmoke*, copyright, 1953, by Flying Eagle Publications, Inc.

Big Ghost Basin, originally published in *Argosy*, copyright, 1951, by Popular Publications, Inc.

The Singing Sands, originally published in *Fifteen Western Tales*, copyright, 1954, by Popular Publications, Inc.

The text of this Large Print edition is unabridged.
Other aspects of the book may vary from the original edition.

Set in 16 pt. New Times Roman.

Printed in Great Britain on acid-free paper.

British Library Cataloguing in Publication Data available

Library of Congress Cataloging-in-Publication Data

Frazee, Steve, 1909–
  The gun-throwers / Steve Frazee.
    p.   cm.
  ISBN 0-7838-8579-2 (lg. print : sc : alk. paper)
  1. Large type books.   I. Title.
[PS3556.R358G86   1999]
813'.54—dc21
                                        99–19638

THE GUN-THROWERS

From the top of Gypsum Hill Hallidane was just a smear at the end of rails which had come from somewhere out of the Texas vastness. Behind his rock, Brett Meredith watched the stage starting up the grade and thought that soon the bigness of the country was going to be mighty handy.

They wouldn't be expecting trouble just a half mile from town, maybe. Not the driver at least, but little Clyde Betters, riding shotgun today, not only expected but pined for trouble every time he went up on the seat.

The business with Betters would have to be timed to the split second. There was plenty of room to bury a man in this country.

The horses were working hard against the grade, the driver was telling a big lie about the women he'd known in El Paso, and Betters seemed to be drowsing when Meredith sprang from cover and yelled, 'Reach, boys!'

The driver locked his wheels, clamped the lines between his knees and reached. Still appearing half asleep Betters flicked his shotgun in line and shot without raising it.

Meredith's timing was right as he dived for cover, but he had no protection against the piece of buck that slammed off a rock and buried itself in the fleshy part of his thigh.

Betters' second barrel took the crown off Meredith's hat as he ducked. It was a flat-crowned hat with a chin thong. He jerked it back in place on his thick thatch of rusty-red hair.

From the rocks on the other side of the stage Jack Sarrett stepped out and called, 'Never mind reloading, Betters! And just leave the carbine where it is.'

With one hand halfway to a carbine in the boot, Betters straightened slowly, his thin face bitter. 'That was the dirtiest trick that was ever pulled on me!' he said.

Sarrett laughed. 'Next time we'll show you a really good one. Live and learn, Betters.' He said to Meredith, 'Get busy while the boys are coming down to stretch their legs. No passengers today.'

The leather-covered box under the driver's boards wasn't heavy. It was easy-to-carry, Meredith thought happily. Sarrett had been right again. But you couldn't trust these Wells Fargo people too far. He smashed the lock and seal with Betters' carbine.

They hadn't been fooling. The contents were crisp and green.

'Got a new partner now, eh, Sarrett?' Betters said.

'You mean Bill? Oh, sure—'

'Bill, hell!' the driver said.

Sarrett laughed, so easily and with so much good humor that Meredith grinned. 'Maybe his name ain't Bill,' Sarrett said. 'You know how those dodgers are—always getting details wrong.' His amused gray eyes watched Meredith a moment. 'That's right, Sam, make sure Betters don't have another gun hid out somewhere.'

After a while Meredith decided the carbine and the empty shotgun seemed to be the size of things. He threw the carbine as far as he could.

Sarrett pointed upgrade with his six-gun. 'Thank you, gentlemen, and goodby!'

They were riding hard for purple hills north of the river when lead sang past and they heard the rifle at the top of Gypsum Hill.

'Told you that Betters was tricky,' Sarrett said. 'He had a long-gun roped somewhere under the coach. Spread!'

The next shot was short, but Betters had the line all right and the line was right at Meredith. It always seemed to be that way, but this time it was probably because his Mexican sorrel made a better target at a distance than Sarrett's gray. He bent low in the saddle and rode, waiting for the next shot.

Sarrett laughed. He laughed any old time, with sand blowing in his face, when he was hungry, with a gun in his guts. 'Over there,' he said. 'The heroes of Hallidane are spurring to the kill.'

Riders drawn by shots were stringing dust from town. Only one went toward the coach;

3

the others cut toward Meredith and Sarrett.

'Lots of fun at one of these riding bees,' Sarrett said.

Betters' third shot made Meredith's horse lunge ahead with a snort. Meredith looked over the leather-covered box under his right arm. The sorrel's rump was bright with blood coming from a streak where the bullet had angled maybe an inch deep.

A minute later they were into a sandy dip and far out of range.

'All right?' Sarrett asked.

'Not good,' Meredith said. 'Now both me and the sorrel are shot in the rump.'

It wasn't really as funny as Sarrett took it.

It wasn't funny at all when the sorrel began to weaken just a little and the riders behind held on.

'Stick to this wash,' Sarrett said. 'I'll swing to the left and take 'em off your tail. See you at Elfego's place tomorrow night.'

Before he put his gray lunging up the bank, Sarrett took the leather box with a casual jerk of his arm.

'Wait a minute! Half of that—'

'Half and the price of a new horse, Brett. Right now you got to ride light. Elfego's tomorrow night. You can find it all right?'

There wasn't time to argue. 'I can find it,' Meredith said. Later, he heard shots and yells from a long way west, so he knew that Sarrett had gone in close enough to make it interesting.

*　　　*　　　*

Meredith reached Elfego's place just after sundown the day after Gypsum Hill. On the edge of the brush, the sprawling collection of weathered *adobe* seemed at the moment to be inhabited only by naked children, goats and chickens. There was an excuse for a corral straddling a little stream. Meredith knew Elfego had other corrals somewhere back in the tangled *brasada*.

A brown lad about fourteen, silver spurs on his bare feet, tremendous buck teeth in his mouth and lots of *sabe* in his liquid eyes, took the Mexican sorrel, glanced at the crusted edges of the wound where vicious flies had gathered, and went toward the brush after nodding toward the largest building.

The buckshot wound felt worse when Meredith started to walk than it had when he was riding. He'd had one canteen of water since yesterday, and he'd used most of it to sponge the sorrel's mouth and nostrils. The sun had burned through the top of his riddled hat and got to his skull in spite of his thick hair. He took the hat off and rubbed a dusty sleeve against his forehead.

There was a hundred-dollar note under the band of that hat. Sarrett had one just like it. It was only common sense, Sarrett always said, to

5

carry a little reserve and never spend it. That way you were never broke.

There would be plenty of notes to carry as soon as Sarrett got here. They could rest their horses until morning and then ride on.

Damn the sun and damn his thirst, Meredith thought as he shook his head to clear it. He stepped over crawling children and dusty hens and went into the largest *adobe*.

Elfego was eating goat stew by himself at a table in the middle of the sprinkled floor. He was naked to the waist, but he had his peaked straw hat on, with the greasy bangs of his curly hair shining darkly against sweat. '*Señor!*' he exclaimed, and pointed to a chair, and went right on eating goat stew.

Meredith had a glass of wine that didn't help his thirst at all. Elfego saw. His big innocent eyes were seeing much. He yelled in Spanish and spewed fragments of peppery stew halfway across the table. An old woman came in with a jug of warm water. About half of it and Meredith thought he felt a little better, even if it didn't take the sun out of his head. He ate some of the goat stew and had to drink the rest of the water quickly.

'And now,' Elfego said some time later, raking delicately between large teeth with a bowie knife that had crusted blood and goat hair against the hilt, 'you have come to visit my poor house. Welcome, *Señor!*'

'How much?' Meredith asked. Sarrett

6

always waited to the end and then paid twice as much as if he'd bargained in the beginning. 'I'll want a lead horse, too—and not one of those scrubs that go blind as soon as they're led out of the brush.'

'Money, *Señor*? Money?' Elfego picked his teeth with one hand and spread the other as if the subject was very boring. 'Later, *Señor*. I see you do not sit well, on the one side only. A little accident, perhaps?'

'Nothing.' The chunk of buck was paining like the devil and his whole thigh was sore.

From the next building came deep laughter, the musical laughter of Mexican girls, and the squeals of children that had been amused by something. Sarrett was probably here already, Meredith thought. People laughed like that when he was around. Even with the detour he had taken, he should have been here first. The long-legged gray was a ground-comber.

'Jack Sarrett over there?' Meredith inclined his head.

Elfego sucked his lips. 'Sarrett? Sarrett? Names, *Señor*, they are nothing at Elfego's.'

'A gray horse, no silver on the saddle. A big man with hair like yours. He laughs so that you would not forget.' What was the use of talking? Meredith would see for himself. He started to rise.

'That one?' Something quick and thoughtful ran in Elfego's eyes. 'No, he is not here.' The thought ran on after his words stopped.

7

'He will be, tonight.'

'Perhaps,' Elfego said. He ticked the point of his knife up and down against the table. 'Now we will talk about money, *Señor*.'

Meredith didn't like the quick change, the insinuation. Where did this stack of lard get the right to hint that Sarrett wouldn't make the rendezvous? 'Tonight will be soon enough,' he said.

'Now, perhaps?' Elfego said politely.

Meredith's chair was clear of the table. He had room to move and he was already leaning a little sidewise to keep weight off his wound. He lifted his right hand off the chair arm. 'Tonight, I said.'

Elfego shrugged. 'Tonight. The house of Elfego is peaceful. We are simple people here.'

And so was anyone who trusted Elfego, Meredith thought. He took a drink of wine and tried to drink away his dizziness.

Elfego cut the piece of buckshot out that night, using his all-purpose knife. Of course he was not skilled, but he was quick and not afraid of cutting.

'Would you like to keep the lead, *Señor*?' he asked. 'It is not a great piece, but—'

'Hell, no!' Meredith said, and grunted when Elfego poured *tequila* into the gash.

Lying on his stomach on a low, flat roof, Meredith watched the moon come up large. It laid clearness on the trail coming up from gray plains that stretched and ran forever into the

8

night. Liquid Spanish and soft music flowed gently, murmuring to the dusk. The complaints of sleepy children finally died away.

Deep laughter mingled with the sounds of women's voices. There were several women here, and few were old. 'My wife's cousins, I think,' Elfego had said. 'So many children, people . . . one cannot remember everything.'

Meredith had seen the men too, long-riders like himself. Sarrett was not among them.

When the wash of moonlight began to die still Sarrett had not come. Meredith drowsed uneasily there on the roof, with his gun beside him. The night was cool but he was hot. Nothing moved on the trail he watched. Toward dawn Elfego's place was quiet. The roof was cold then.

Sarrett had not come. He might have got hit drawing the pursuers off, Meredith thought; or he might have been forced to lay low somewhere else. He would be here.

Elfego woke him when the light was gray. The Mexican was standing below, at the end of the building, with the strong smell of him drifting up. From near the brush came the sounds of footsteps and a soft curse as men moved away into the thickets.

Meredith's hat was right where he had left it, with his arm across it.

'You will ride now,' Elfego said. 'The sheriff comes from Hallidane with men.'

Meredith came down from the roof. He was

burning with fever and shaking at the same time. 'I'll wait for Sarrett.'

'*Sí, sí!* But not at my poor *jacal*. If you stay you must wait in the Pit.'

Meredith had heard of the Pit, a hole scooped out somewhere back in the brush. It was said that two wounded men hidden there by Elfego had been torn to pieces by *javelinas*.

'Not the Pit.'

Elfego kept glancing into the grayness. 'If you cannot ride, there is no other place. The sheriff sometimes leaves men here for three days. Like pigs they eat. It is a small price I must pay—'

'I want a lead horse, a good one. The sorrel will be stiff for a while—'

'You have money?'

'Damn you, no! But later—'

'I could trade for the sorrel, but . . . ah, the poor horse! So badly wounded—'

'The hell it is! In a week's time—'

'The horse may die soon.' Elfego sighed. 'But I am a generous man. I, Elfego, will trade my best mare for this poor dying sorrel only because—'

The noise of distant hooves came from the trail that led toward the plains.

'The sorrel and fifty dollars,' Elfego said.

'I'll stay and fight it out with the sheriff,' Meredith said. The way he felt he didn't care.

Elfego groaned. 'My best mare gone for a crippled horse. This is what happens when a

10

poor man—'

'Move!' Meredith ordered.

They did not go all the way to the corral. In a small open space a few hundred feet back in the brush the same bucktoothed boy who had led the sorrel away was waiting with a saddled mare, a potbellied *sabino*.

'My poor Conchita, my lovely horse, I grieve . . .' Elfego put his arms around the mare's neck and she staggered.

It was the worst kind of robbery. Meredith drew his gun. 'We'll go to the corral,' he said.

From the houses a deep voice ran out over the thickets. 'Tom! Take two men in to check the corrals. They'll be moved again, but have a look.'

Time had run out. Meredith swung up on the *sabino* and the animal sighed at the weight.

'Go north, *Señor*,' Elfego said. 'Go with God.'

'Go to hell!' Meredith said, and rode off in a warped saddle on a rack of bones. The bucktoothed lad had already slipped away to take the sorrel where no posse would find it.

The pink mare had dropped somewhere from old age and exhaustion, and Meredith was stumbling through *agrito*, trying to curse, his body a world of fever and weariness, when he remembered one bright thing from the whole mess—the hundred-dollar note. Catclaw raked his back as he slumped down to have a look. His hands were big and fumbly,

11

unusually slow for *his* hands. His clothes were torn. His eyes were red hot and sheets of grayness kept rushing across his vision.

It was a long time before he knew he didn't have the note. Gone with everything else, stolen when he lay asleep on Elfego's roof so long ago.

He stumbled on, with thorns ripping and sticking in flesh where other thorns had already ripped and stuck. There was only one way, just cover your face with your arms and bull ahead. He fell and tasted blood on his arms where flies were working. His gun was a terrible weight, but he wouldn't drop it. He didn't dare drop it.

Where ghost-gray trees stood gaunt around a blinding open place he fell and crawled, and then he could not crawl any more.

Elfego was stealing his gun, the last thing he had of any value. Meredith tried to fight him off, but he couldn't talk and he couldn't see. And suddenly it was all over.

He woke up four days later. He saw pecan ceiling beams above him and through a low window set in stone the blunt rise and fall of the *brasada* with the setting sun on it.

'Well, stranger, I thought you were young and tough.'

There was an old man in the low-ceilinged room, a stringy old cuss with bright brown eyes that moved as quickly as a road-runner. Maybe he wasn't so old, at that, Meredith decided after he had a better look. It was just that the mark of the brush was on him, the same lean, tough, weathered look that grows on a brushpopping steer.

'Picked you up in the salt bed on my way from town,' the old boy said. 'Have a drink of this.' It was *huisache* tea, and Meredith was to drink a lot of it before he could defend himself.

'Town?' he asked.

'Mesa Vaca.'

That was a long way from Hallidane, at least. Meredith closed his eyes again. Later that evening the old man fed him some wild *chiltipiquines*. 'Best thing in the world for fever, or anything else. You had a bad time, son, even after I got you here.'

Meredith knew that when he tried to get up the next day and couldn't make it.

He stayed almost a month with old Andy McRae. At first he thought any man who would live alone in this place was crazy—ticks and heat and thickets all around, and wild bulls that bellowed in the evening at the waterhole below the stone house. McRae owned two thousand acres of brush and he didn't know how many steers, nor was it likely that all the riders in Texas could ever have choused them out to tally.

Later, Meredith decided that the place wasn't too bad. It was cool sometimes in the evening. If a man got to know the brush . . .

13

well, maybe after you got as old as McRae it might be all right.

'I'll be drifting in a day or two, Andy,' he said one night. He had to find Sarrett, who would be looking for him, too, get his share of the loot from Gypsum Hill—and then he'd try to pay old Andy for what he'd done.

'Sure, son.' Andy sucked his pipe and nodded. Then he got up and took a piece of paper from a cupboard. As dodgers go, it was a good picture of Meredith and Sarrett standing together at a hitchrack before a Comanche Wells saloon. Sarrett had been laughing at the way the traveling photographer went under his dusty black cloth. The dodger said Sarrett was worth three hundred dollars more than Meredith.

'Quite a boy, that Sarrett,' McRae said. 'The day after him and—somebody—outfoxed Clyde Betters at Gypsum Hill, Sarrett took a stage west of Comanche for thirteen thou—'

'West of Comanche!' Meredith stared into McRae's live brown eyes. That meant that Sarrett had ridden like the very devil to get there the day after Gypsum Hill.

'It was a well planned business,' McRae said, and went on to describe it.

After a few moments Meredith wasn't listening. That second robbery had been set up at least a week in advance, from what McRae said. Sarrett never had intended to go to Elfego's. *'Right now you got to ride light,'* he'd

14

said when he took the money. Sure, he'd led the posse away from Meredith, but he'd had to cross their route anyway to get where he'd been headed all the time.

Anger thumped and churned in Meredith. There wasn't a ten-year-old kid in Texas half as simple as he'd been. Elfego had known all the time after Sarrett's name was mentioned. Sitting there belching at his table he'd been able to guess the truth in a second. Meredith thought of the hours he'd spent lying on the roof, watching, waiting, afraid that Sarrett had run into hard luck.

And then on top of everything, Elfego had pulled *his* whizzer. But Sarrett was the cause of it all.

'Got it all figured out?' McRae asked.

'Including the killing.'

'Big order, of course,' McRae said mildly. 'The last the Rangers heard of Sarrett he'd crossed into Oklahoma. They got the man that took the big chance on the job west of Comanche. Got him the hard way.'

'Naturally they got him,' Meredith said bitterly. 'Can you trust me for a saddle and horse?'

'We can fix up something. I been trading around a little while you were learning to walk—' He stopped when he saw how Meredith resented a glance at his thigh.

The next day he took Meredith back into the brush a piece. McRae, also, had a corral

15

not too close to his house. In it was Meredith's Mexican sorrel, and under a tarp in a shed was Meredith's saddle and bridle. McRae looked embarrassed. 'I know Elfego pretty well, know how to straighten him out now and then. I—well—there's your damned stuff, kid. The sorrel's good as ever now.'

What Elfego had done to Meredith didn't seem so important now. Greed walks with any man. But Sarrett—he had made a damned fool of a friend. *You got to ride light,'* he'd said, and he'd been laughing to himself.

'You know,' McRae said, 'I'd just forget about Sarrett. Say you were lucky enough to catch him and fast enough to blast him—it wouldn't do you any good. He'd go out laughing at you. That's the way he's made.'

'You know him?'

'He's stopped here. I never seen a man I liked as much and trusted as little as Jack Sarrett. Take that business of carrying a hundred-dollar bill in his hat. He never did in his life. He spends money so fast he never even gets into his pockets, let alone in his hat. But he's talked plenty of suckers into carrying a big bill in their hats, just so's he or somebody else could steal it.'

Meredith was glad McRae was looking into the catclaw at the moment.

'No,' McRae said, 'killing him wouldn't give a man much satisfaction—and it would be a big order too.'

'Every wolf has its bullet.'

'I wouldn't bother with him, son.'

'Thanks—for advice I don't need.'

'I didn't either, when I was your age,' McRae said. 'Going after him ain't a question of what it's going to do to him; it's a question of what it's going to do to you.'

Meredith didn't understand and he didn't care to. He said, 'I'll take care of myself.'

Before he crossed the Brazos he was doubly sure his way was best. A long day's ride always pained him—the results of Betters' shotgun, Elfego's filthy knife, and Sarrett's doublecross were concentrated in one place. While no man watching him ride could have guessed he pained, whenever Meredith went up in the saddle he was reminded that he must seek vengeance.

It was worse than mangled ears that showed a gunslinger had made a fool of you. You could wear your ears down the street in plain sight and let your eyes dare any man to look too long or make a crack.

In Fort Worth he knocked a saddlemaker off the walk when the man, after watching Meredith get stiffly from his horse, suggested that the saddle didn't fit him.

He crossed the Big Red and at a small tent town on Little Red got his first news of Sarrett. Crooked land speculators had worked railroad talk to a frenzy and had reaped a fine harvest selling lots the month before. And then the

17

assistant to the chief surveyor of the railroad arrived, got chummy with the speculators, and for an undisclosed sum tipped them off to exactly where the railroad was going to run.

The speculators rushed south to the promised land and bought up the farms of two startled farmers who had just about starved out. There were even a few survey stakes around to sustain the wild buying. Immediately the assistant to the chief surveyor, a big, curly-haired man who laughed a lot and spent money freely, went away to get his parties organized and working full swing.

It was some time before the speculators learned that they had cornered land in a country where no railroad ever would run.

'You'd'a laughed yourself sick to hear them sharks howl,' a bartender told Meredith. 'Can't say that I can blame 'em for being took in, either. This Meredith was a man I'd'a trusted—'

'Who?'

'Brett Meredith, the fellow as said he was the surveyor. Looked like a Longhorn to me.'

'Yeah,' Meredith said, and drank his whiskey at a gulp, sand and all. 'Yeah, I guess I would have laughed myself sick. I wonder where this—Meredith—went from here?'

'Nobody knows.' The bartender blew some of the sand off a dirty glass and set it on the plank bar. 'But a man like that will be heard from again, I'll bet.'

Meredith didn't know which way to go. He sort of favored Texas, figuring that by now Sarrett had slipped back. Rangers wouldn't worry him too much. They never had.

The twenty dollars McRae had given him had taken him a long way, but he was flat now. Buzzer, the Mexican sorrel, had to eat and so did Brett Meredith. He took a dry, empty stomach a long way to where he'd heard of a trail drive. Tol Carruthers, the topscrew, looked him over and said he didn't need any hands. 'That is, unless—' the drover boss shook his head doubtfully—'you wanted to take the wagon. The cook's rheumatics put him flat two weeks ago on the other side of the Red. It was mainly just not wanting to leave Texas, I think.'

'I'll take it,' Meredith said, and that was another disgrace to score against Sarrett, who was somewhere fat as a feeder steer and laughing his head off. 'Where in Kansas?'

'To the Platte—that's up in Nebraska.' Carruthers looked at the way Meredith wore his gun. 'Never been out of Texas before, huh?'

'That,' said Meredith, 'is none of your damned business.'

'You sound like a cook already,' the foreman said. 'Camp in an hour. We're going to be mighty hungry.'

Meredith was mighty hungry at the moment. It was probably colder than Alaska

19

up in Nebraska, but it might be as good a place as any to look for Sarrett.

By the time he'd crossed Kansas he had almost learned to cook. He took a lot of ragging, not all good-natured, about his efforts. He took nothing the morning he rolled from under the wagon with his hip hurting from a night in blankets soaked by rain that had washed against him.

'Got lead in your pants this morning, Gimpy?' Hod Oliver asked.

Meredith took off his apron. His cedar-handled Colt was where he always wore it, even while cooking. He faced Oliver and the rest eating around the fire. 'What was that you asked?'

They looked at his blocky face and his narrowed eyes. Oliver had trouble swallowing a mouthful of flapjacks. 'No offense, Cookie,' he said. 'I pass the hand.'

For Texans, they were even careful in the remarks they made about his cooking after that.

Meredith was surprised to find no snow in Nebraska in early September. In fact, he thought it hotter there than in many parts of Texas. Folks in the little railroad town where the drive ended were laughing about something that had happened over at Ryepatch that summer. A saloonman there had paid eight dollars a head for a thousand steers, received a bill of sale and taken a couple of drinks when the seller set up the house to celebrate the deal.

The only hitch was that the cattle, bedded down just a quarter of a mile away, had not belonged to the seller.

'What did the fellow look like?' Meredith asked a bartender.

'Like the man who owned the herd. He rode right over from the drive while the others was getting the steers bedded down, only it turns out later that he'd been riding with 'em only a few miles. Well, anyone sucker enough to think he could buy at eight dollars a head . . .'

Meredith drew half his pay. He told Carruthers to send the rest to a man named Andy McRae at Mesa Vaca when the Texans got as close as they would go to the place.

Carruthers said, 'It gets mighty cold up here, I've heard.'

'I can stand it if he can.'

Carruthers didn't ask who. He said, 'I thought it was like that. See you in Texas, kid.'

The saloonkeeper in Ryepatch was very sour about the ranicaboo he'd stepped into, but he had to justify his error. 'This Clyde Betters had the marks of the long haul all over him. He was dry, too.' The saloonman shook his hand at Meredith. 'A man comes in here with a herd bawling and kicking dust so close I could have hit 'em with an empty bottle. He says he owns that herd and wants to do business before he gets so drunk he ain't

21

responsible. These yahoos around here are laughing now, but not one of them that was here at the time and drunk the whiskey this Betters set up to 'em thought he was anything but what—'

'A big black-haired man, laughed with his eyes so you had to laugh with him, gray eyes?'

'That's him!' The saloonman added darkly, 'A friend of yours?'

'No friend of mine.'

'I'll stand a drink on that. I need one every time I think about him.'

'Any idea which way this—Betters—went?'

The saloonman grunted and gave that question the silence it deserved.

Meredith sat into a stud game. He needed enough money to finance his search for a while without having to be slowed down by working. In a half hour he was broke. There wasn't much to being honest, he thought. He got his horse and ground-hitched it at the side of the bank. They were shoveling around a lot of money in there. Just a couple of pocketsful out of the teller's window near the door would be all he needed.

He rolled a cigarette and waited for customers to clear out of the bank. People scuffing through the dust didn't pay much attention to him until a little man with eyes like Clyde Betters' walked up and stuck a gun in his back. Suspicious people here in Nebraska, Meredith thought. He hadn't even robbed the bank yet.

Across the street another man with a badge stepped out from between two buildings. He had a rifle.

The marshal behind Meredith said, 'You seen that sign that says Texans don't carry guns in Ryepatch?'

'No,' Meredith lied, and breathed easier.

'Too bad,' the marshal said.

The marshal wasn't downright mean. After Meredith got out of jail sometime later he helped the Texan find a job on a ranch forty miles west on the river. It was the worst winter Meredith ever put in. The longhorns drifted into fence corners, piled up and froze, and Meredith almost did, in spite of shotgun chaps, a woman's shawl under his hat and—worst of all—bulky overshoes on top of his boots. His wound ached something fierce every time he got into a frosty saddle. Buzzer didn't like the winter either.

O Lord! What an awful score there was against Jack Sarrett.

Sometimes in spite of himself Meredith jerked open the door of the miserable sod hut they called a line shanty in this north country and stared into blizzards to see if he really had heard Sarrett laughing out there. But he knew Jack Sarrett had not been trapped in the cold, not him. He was in some warm *cantina*, far away from air that struck like a knife.

Spring came at last and there wasn't a

bluebonnet in sight, just sand and dirty brown grass.

In Ryepatch Meredith got half of his winter's wages changed into one note. He gave a milliner a dollar to put some oiled silk around it and sew it under the sweatband of his hat. He'd break into that hundred dollars to celebrate right after he gunned Jack Sarrett kicking.

Here and there on his way toward the Red, Meredith saw *Wanted* sheets with the same picture McRae had shown him in the *brasada*. He was glad that he'd only trimmed the beard he'd grown for warmth that winter in the snow.

Down in the southern hills of Oklahoma, where people said the winter had been mild, a big, popular, laughing man named Starr had run a saloon for a few weeks until, tiring of it, he had given it to the bartender and ridden away singing. The women in the town, married and unmarried, had thought well of Starr, even if he had been a saloonkeeper.

Not far across the Texas line Meredith made up to a dancehall woman to see if he couldn't get some news of Sarrett. She didn't know or wouldn't talk about the man, but she did warm up to Meredith enough to warn him that two tough deputy sheriffs were just about to snap up a red-headed man who owned a Mexican sorrel.

It was close. Buzzer split a lot of Texas air before Meredith got back across the line. He got to figuring that if he, who hadn't owned much of a record at all before he joined up with Sarrett, could attract so much law-dog lead, Sarrett would be good for much more. The laughing man was no fool in spite of his arrogant carelessness.

He was probably letting crime in Texas limp along without him.

Out in western Oklahoma Meredith heard about the stage that had been robbed in a gully east of Red Feather that spring. At dusk one evening the stage had come against large rocks piled across the road where a sign burned into a wagon board said: BRIDGE BUSTED.

The guard, driver and passengers argued about the sign and the bridge half a mile away. In the end the driver followed a promising detour because it showed fresh marks of several wagons. The stage was robbed of fifteen thousand dollars after it was hopelessly stuck in a gully. Not one got a good look at the man in the dark, but everyone heard him laugh as he gave orders to four confederates stationed with rifles along the sides of the trap. Some passengers said seven confederates.

Daylight showed the tracks of only one horse—and three piles of brush that had been set against the skyline to look like men with rifles. Daylight also showed a broken-down wagon that had been run many times over the false detour, making it look well traveled.

Sarrett must have really laughed about that

one, Meredith thought grimly. He was beginning to worry about Sarrett a little. The man would make a mistake and get killed.

Reliable information from people who were authorities on the Red Feather job indicated seven directions in which Meredith's man had gone.

A cowboy with a rusty-red thatch of hair, a short beard and a look in his eye came into Granada, Colorado, that fall on a Mexican sorrel with a gray scar welt on its rump. He watched other cowboys welcome in a train by trying to shoot the headlight out, and learned that Curly Elfego, a laughing man from Oklahoma, had introduced the pastime one day when things were dull.

It was also in Granada, when two saloonmen were warring verbally, threatening to blow each other's places sky-high, that someone rolled an immense, spitting bomb into the Plains Palace one night. Windows and closed doors and other fragile barriers that impeded egress went out with the crowd, and soon the place was deserted except for a dancehall girl who had been knocked under a table and who was too scared to move but scared enough to remember a prayer.

The bomb made a lot of smoke that fogged the interior. The dancehall girl, between prayers, watched Curly Elfego moving unhurriedly but efficiently as he raked into a gunnysack abandoned money from the

26

cashier's doghouse and the bar tills. Later, the girl forgot her praying and used other language that came more naturally. She threw a pail of beer on the bomb, which turned out to be a large, black-painted wooden ball with a burned-out fuse.

Again, Meredith had his choice of many directions. He was a month behind.

The man who stopped beside Meredith in front of the Queen one night had all the looks of a smoky trail behind him, a tight mouth, wary eyes and a face that was not easy to read.

'Looking for a man?' he asked.

'I didn't say so.'

'No, but for two days you've sure swiveled your ears like a deer when a certain name was mentioned.'

Meredith's face and eyes were hard.

'I figured I was about two thousand ahead when Curly Elfego rolled that phony bomb into the Palace,' the man said. 'Only time I ever win in my whole life. I picked up my chips, but by the time I got out I'd been shoved and tromped so much I didn't have a single counter left.'

'Too bad.'

'Yeah, only I mean it. This Curly—I heard him tell a woman he was on his way to Juarez. Had a deal there. Said he could pass as a Mex when he wanted to.'

'I didn't ask about Curly Elfego,' Meredith said. He thought he knew a blazer when he heard one.

'You sure didn't,' the man said, and started away.

'Who was the woman?' Meredith asked.

'Pearl. The only good looking one at the Queen.'

She was that, all right. Meredith already had tried to pump her about Sarrett, and got nowhere at all. Women were like that after Jack Sarrett had passed through their lives. This time he didn't rush things. Down on the Pecos nobody had called him an open-mouthed jinglebob around women from the time he was sixteen.

He sold the lead horse he'd picked up on his way across Kansas and spent almost all the money on Pearl. He had three fights before a few hardheads admitted he was the fair-haired boy for the moment. She liked him too, he decided. She even told him the giveaway signs of a blackjack dealer in the Queen, so he was able to make several minor killings and buy the lead horse back. Pearl talked him into shaving his beard, and he didn't mind that either, because he was a long way from the last dodger he'd seen with his picture on it.

But he couldn't waste too much time. One night he asked, 'I wonder where old Curly ever went from here?'

Pearl stiffened just a little, and then she got a sort of dreamy look in her eye, like a lot of women who had known Sarrett.

'I guess he drifted back to Nebraska, probably,' Meredith said.

'I suppose. He said he always liked it there.'

Meredith knew he wasn't going to get anyplace playing the edges. Pearl was pretty fond of him in her way, and she couldn't know who he was; so he jumped right into the middle. 'Did he ever mention going to Juarez?'

If he hadn't been watching so closely he never would have seen the flick of caution in her eyes or her split-second hesitation. 'No,' she said. 'He mentioned going lots of places, but I'm sure Juarez wasn't one of them.'

It was good enough for Meredith. He rode south that afternoon with enough money to see him through. No one in Raton was very communicative, but finally a stable hostler admitted that a big, laughing man with curly black hair had been there the month before.

In Las Vegas, Meredith had to go into Old Town and take his chances before he found a loafer who had seen Sarrett only three weeks before. Because it offered a large field for Sarrett's talent, Albuquerque was probably the man's next stop, Meredith reasoned. So he cut southwest instead to see if he couldn't pick up time.

He had a rough two weeks on Chupadera Mesa, got lost, nearly died of thirst, took an Apache arrow in the arm, and lost his lead horse. But nothing could stop him now. Even

29

Buzzer, gaunt and weary, seemed to know that at last they were closing.

Meredith reached Lava Butte. He was thin, grim and dried out like old leather. No one in Lava Butte admitted they had seen his man.

The sheriff at Las Cruces, almost to the border, sized Meredith up keenly during his first half hour in town. He looked at the sorrel and seemed satisfied.

'You're Brett Meredith, ain't you?' he asked.

Meredith nodded, his mind and muscles ready. He'd never shot a badge-toter yet, but nobody was going to stop him.

'Got a message for you,' the sheriff said. 'C'mon.'

Meredith went warily. The officer took a dirty piece of paper from a desk drawer and handed it over.

'BRIDGE OUT,' it read, 'but since you've gone that far, why not visit Juarez anyway?' It was signed, *Jack*.

'Mex riding through give it to me last week,' the lawman said.

For a while Meredith wouldn't believe what he knew was sure. All he could think of was about the Apaches that had almost got him, of days without water—and of how Sarrett must be laughing. He choked as he asked, 'This Mex—what did he look like?'

'Maybe fifty, go 'bout a hundred and ten, spoke fair English—' He watched Meredith sink into a chair. 'Too much sun, maybe?'

Meredith was sick all right. It had been a typical Sarrett trick from scratch. That tight-mouthed man in Granada couldn't have made it stick alone . . . but Pearl . . . she'd cinched it with just a tiny bit of acting. And those people he thought he'd so cleverly searched out along the way—they'd been paid off by the little Mexican to keep Meredith going. Sarrett was laughing himself sick.

The sheriff, of course, didn't understand, but he was sympathetic. 'Lots of officers have missed by closer than you, son.'

Being called a lawman piled on more than Meredith thought he could bear. He staggered outside where the hot strike of the afternoon sun reminded him again of what he'd been through.

'Better rest up,' the sheriff said. 'You're fearful gaunted. What's the matter there with your rear? You keep a-rubbing—'

'I got it caught in a bear trap!' Meredith said savagely. 'When I was poking into other folks' business!'

He left without filling his canteens, but after a few miles he realized he wasn't going to get back to Granada at that pace.

It took him five months to get back. He had to work where he could, once on a railroad carrying green ties with Mexican laborers. He never thought of spending the hundred in his hat, a different hat now. That money was still for celebrating right after his wolf had caught its bullet.

Long ago he had ruled against using his guns for easy passage. Three weeks in the Ryepatch jail had taught him how bad it would be if he slipped on a job and was put away somewhere to reflect for years on a mission unfulfilled.

Pearl was still at the Queen when Meredith rode into Granada one bitter day with the wind whipping dust and dry snow against his ragged clothes.

Her face got a little pale, but her eyes were unafraid. She shrugged away a tall cowboy, who stepped a little farther aside when he saw Meredith's face. She led Meredith to her room to talk, and they did not speak a word on the way. He'd never beaten a woman the way he was going to beat her. He'd slapped down wildcats in *cantinas* when they tried to knife him, but this had to be better than a casual wallop.

'You might have found him if I hadn't helped send you down there,' she said, so matter-of-factly that he was stopped for a moment. 'I don't know what it is that sends you after Jack Sarrett, but I know it can't be worth it to you. It's made you so bitter you aren't young.'

'You helped age me.' He'd spent his twenty-third birthday on Chupadera, beside a dead horse, with Apaches trying to work in to finish

32

him. 'You helped do that! You lied to me right!'

'I lied, of course, but not for money like the rest. The twelve days I knew Jack Sarrett meant something to me that you couldn't understand. I was never so happy and laughed so much in my life—and I knew all the time he'd ride away when he wanted to. And if I knew where he was right now, I'd lie to you again.'

She grabbed a two-barreled derringer from under a dirty pillow and stood with it at her side. 'Now, if you're still set on showing what a big fierce man you are—start!'

She wasn't bluffing, he knew. He also knew he could get her wrist before she had the derringer all the way up.

'So you love the no good son!' he snarled.

'That's none of your damned business! At least, he never set out to kill a man. You're a dirty killer at heart, Brett Meredith. Jack's just out for the laughs there are in life.'

She sat down on the bed suddenly and let the gun drop on a scrap of dust-covered faded green carpet. Here and there she'd made a stab to pretty up the place, but it was just like a hundred other rooms Meredith had seen in places like the Queen.

He drew a deep breath and glared at her. She wasn't even looking at him now, just sitting there with her mouth screwed up, her face not very clean, her eyes staring at the floor. Even then she was a handsome girl, and she was younger than he; but there wasn't much chance that she'd be either young or good looking very long.

She'd lied about Sarrett to Meredith, and now for the rest of her life she'd lie to herself about those twelve days with Jack Sarrett.

Meredith knew that as he stood there with his eyes bloodshot from dust and cold, with his hard, whiskered jaw tightening his mouth. He told himself he ought to knock her around until she couldn't go out on the floor for a month.

But all he did was walk from the room and leave her sitting there staring at a faded scrap of carpet in a dirty, cold room where wind was pushing sand past warping window frames.

He stopped in a town on the Arkansas where rattlesnakes outnumbered other inhabitants, a town with a brand new church that had been donated by a traveling minister named Jonathan Starr.

'He was a handsome man with a vital, stirring appearance,' a woman member of the congregation told Meredith, 'and he wasn't afraid of an honest laugh. Of course, when we discovered that the lumber he donated for the church really belonged to the Santa Fe railroad, it was embarrassing.' She rallied and went on staunchly. 'But I'm sure Reverend Starr confused the pile with some that he had ordered.'

'Uh-uh, so am I. And where is the Reverend Starr now, do you know?'

'He said he was going north to carry the Message to Blackfoot Indians in Montana.'

Lord help the Blackfeet! Meredith thought.

Montana was a long ride away. Meredith didn't get there until spring. His man had been in Hardin in the fall. A saloonman who had fallen for the old buried Spanish treasure trick testified to that.

It was a long time later before Meredith again heard of Sarrett. The redhead was riding shotgun on a stage-line out of Larned, making a living and hoping that someday the right robber would step out to make his play. Meredith had gone Clyde Betters one better. In spring clips on the floor of the stage he'd rigged a carbine and practiced until he could use his toe to flip it into his hands in no time if he ever needed backing for his shotgun.

Meredith was in love with Mary Linford then, daughter of the stage-line owner.

She'd been alone in the office the day he'd dropped in to look at pictures in the hope of finding news of Sarrett. He was dusty and his clothes were in bad shape, and never in his life had he been so aware of his appearance when Mary smiled at him.

'Just wanted to look at the pictures over there, ma'am.'

'Go right ahead,' she said, and smiled again.

He thumbed past the old one of himself and

Sarrett before he realized. She wasn't like a lot he'd seen, so bright-pretty it smacked you right in the face. Her hair was kind of pale blond and not wavy at all. She was a slender girl, and he'd seen many with better curves, or at least more of them. It was her eyes and her smile, some kind of cleanness that ran all the way through her being.

All at once, even though he knew he was going to ride away soon and never see her again, he wanted to get rid of the circular of him and Sarrett. He got it when two men came into the office, one a blunt-jawed man who looked like he could use the gun on his hip, the other a slender youth in dark broadcloth.

The smile that Mary gave the youth was considerably different from the one she'd given Meredith, and it made him look a second time at the young whelp in broadcloth.

'I was thinking, Mary,' the youth said, 'that maybe Bart here would do for the guard your father wants.'

'He might. Why don't you ask Dad, Roger?'

'Well, you know . . . your word with him . . .'

'After all, Roger, Dad is the boss.'

'I know, but . . . well, all right, we'll ask your father.'

The youth was not quite man-size, Meredith decided. He'd sounded like a kid who wanted to whine a little after his mother refused a favor, but was afraid to.

Meredith went over to the counter. 'You

36

need a stage guard?'

'Yes.' She sized him up, and he knew that she was seeing plenty.

'I need a job, and I can handle it.' Her eyes were the clearest he'd ever seen, a sort of hazel with green flecks in them. They looked at him for what seemed a long time.

'You're hired,' she said, and only then did she glance at the door and let her eyes say that she trusted him not to shoot off his mouth.

D. C. Linford never knew but that he had done the hiring himself when he came in a half hour later. Meredith wasn't simple enough to think he'd charmed the girl, and he wasn't surprised at all to find out later that Bart was considered unreliable because of whiskey, or that he owed Roger Hammond's father money.

The weeks rolled with the stages. Meredith had enough money to go on with his search, but he told himself he needed more; and besides, maybe Sarrett would come to him if he just waited long enough.

He didn't exactly dislike Roger Hammond, the only son of one of the town's leading merchants, but he did consider the youth a poor excuse for Mary, even if it was foregone that the two were to be married some day. Hammond wasn't much. He'd have been in the way in Chupadera and other places. But he had the stability of a town around him and money behind him, so maybe he'd be all right.

Meredith got to take Mary to dances several times when Roger was busy at the store. Finally the guard decided that Hammond wasn't going to have her at all. He began to tell himself that Mary's smile carried for him the same message it did for Roger Hammond.

One night when he was driving her home from a dance out in the country under starlight so bright he could have shot a tomato can at twenty paces, he stopped the buggy and said abruptly, 'I've been saving my money.'

'I know,' she said, 'and I think it's fine.'

Nothing that had worked with other girls was any good now. The old, easy ways didn't even come to his mind.

'Look, Mary, the day I first saw you there in the office, when you trusted me without asking a single question, I—' He took a deep breath and looked at her face tilted up in the starlight. 'I love you, Mary—something awful.'

'I know.' There was a sadness in her voice that chilled him. 'I'm going to marry Roger, Brett.'

'Why? He hasn't got—' He almost made the mistake of saying what he thought of Roger Hammond.

'I know he hasn't been hardened by trial as you have. I know you look down on him because he hasn't done the same things you have. But I love him and I'm going to marry him.'

He didn't remember starting the horse.

'What's wrong with me, Mary?'

'Nothing. You're as fine a man as I've ever known. Some girl will be mighty lucky—'

Some girl! Lord help him, there was only one girl in the world.

He stopped the horse again. 'Look, if it's anything in my past that's hurting me, I'll tell you every—'

'No, Brett, it's nothing in your past, and if I loved you I'd marry you and never ask about your past.'

'It is my past!'

She shook her head. 'No. I told the same thing to Jack Sarrett, and he believed—'

'Jack Sarrett!'

'I'll tell you everything now. He was here last summer. He came into the office his first few minutes in town, just as you did. Only he was sizing things up for a robbery. He told me afterward. Jack Sarrett stayed in Larned all summer and made Roger so jealous he couldn't sleep nights.'

'Jack Sarrett wanted to marry you?' Meredith choked back a curse.

'I finally convinced him I was going to marry Roger.'

'Why, that Sarrett is the biggest outlaw—'

'I know. He told me everything. He told me about you, too. He said you'd be the bitterest, grimmest man I'd ever seen, and at first I thought he was right, but you've shed a lot of that since you've been here. Don't put it on

39

again, Brett.'

'Didn't the marshal—somebody—recognize—'

'He's changed a lot since that picture of you two—the picture you ripped away your first day in the office—was taken at Comanche Wells. Both of you have changed. Jack Sarrett lived quietly here. He bought a livery stable. He was well liked and popular.'

Before they reached the lights ahead, Meredith stopped the buggy again. 'Mary, this Hammond is no man for you. If it ever gets rough after you're married, you're going to have to carry the two of you.'

'I know that,' she said. 'I love him, that's all.'

It was all.

Meredith got Buzzer from the stable the next morning. He told D. C. Linford he was leaving. The old man's eyes were wise with knowledge he didn't speak. 'You were the best man I ever had,' he said. 'Come back any time.'

Meredith hadn't intended to see Mary again, but he had to. She was alone in the office, just as she'd been that day when dreams that would never be again had started to rise in a dusty, grim man.

'Don't go on and wreck your life doing something about a long-ago wrong that doesn't matter now,' she told him.

'Will you marry me?'

'Please, Brett, let's not start that again.'

40

'All right! You're the only person in the world that could have stopped me from killing Jack Sarrett, but since you want him killed—'

She didn't say, 'You're being childish.' He was and he knew it. She shook her head at him gently and smiled.

'Good-by, Mrs. Hammond!' he said, and left her. The last he saw of Mary Linford she was standing at the window watching him mount Buzzer.

She waved as he rode away. He did not wave back.

He rode into a loneliness as big as the winds and plains ahead. For a while he hadn't been alone, but now he had no one to talk to, no place to run for refuge. Days later the worst scalding bitterness was gone, and he wished then that he had been a man those last few moments in the office. He wished, too, that he had smiled and waved at her in leaving.

The only consolation that he had was that Jack Sarrett, for once, had been stopped cold. The filthy, clever son, trying to sell himself to Mary by pretending that he was in love with her. But it hadn't got him anyplace.

For once Meredith could laugh at *him*. But the trouble was he could not laugh at all.

In Dodge City he picked up Sarrett's trail again. This time it led into Wyoming.

Nights crouched beside far campfires with him. Days mocked him with their brightness. He had time to twist his thinking to suit his purpose, and there was no one to challenge his devious reasoning. Long before he reached Cheyenne he had charged his loss of Mary to Sarrett.

Sarrett had been in Cheyenne. He had allowed himself to be drawn into a senseless gunfight and killed two local toughs. The affair puzzled Meredith because it was unlike Jack Sarrett, who had always let force be his tool without actually using it. It was odd, too, that no one seemed to remember Sarrett for his laughing.

In Great Falls, Montana, Meredith lost the trail entirely. It was more than three years before he picked it up again. Necessity trapped him one winter near Fort Benton. Toward spring, when the madness of inaction was upon him, he stood in the doorway of a pole cabin, looking at a snow-locked range with dying cattle, and cursed the weather as he cursed Sarrett, and prayed for a chinook as he prayed to find Sarrett.

He tried Wyoming again, Nebraska, and Oklahoma, watching the towns where the big drives came through. And then he heard from a man in Kansas that Sarrett was dead.

He wouldn't believe it.

He heard it again from a Texan he'd known long before.

'Three, four years back,' the fellow said. 'The Rangers got him.'

Sarrett was dead! Meredith had been

robbed. He wasn't quite sane when he began to believe. He got violently drunk in Abilene, and would have killed three men who crossed him. A barkeeper reached out with a shotgun and dented the barrels on Meredith's head. The marshal returned his gun at the edge of town and pointed toward the road. Before Meredith reached Larned on his way to Texas to get the details of Sarrett's death, he bought new clothes.

Old D. C. Linford said that Mary and her husband were now somewhere in Colorado. Hammond's father was dead, the business sold, and the couple had gone to the mountains where Roger was going to make a fortune mining.

'I ain't heard from her in three years,' Linford said. 'It ain't good with her, or she'd have wrote.' He shook his head. 'A fellow was here several months back asking about her. Asked about you too. Jack Sarrett, but when I knew him before his name—'

'Sarett was here? A few months ago?'

Meredith finally reached the Denver address from which Linford had last heard of his daughter. It was a hotel. Nobody remembered the Hammonds or Sarrett.

Mining, Meredith thought. That's what Hammond had come for. He was somewhere in the mountains, and somewhere close was Sarrett, trailing along, trying to cause trouble, not satisfied with his rebuff.

Meredith didn't like the mountains worth a damn, but where Sarrett went . . .

Just before spring, at an Indian agency somewhere near the Cochetopa, he was ready to turn back and again try the camps near Denver. The agent said that Zebulon Valley, on west, had no towns and no people except a few fool prospectors that likely had frozen by now.

'Coldest valley in America,' the agent said. 'Your breath freezes right in your mouth. Last fall the government sent a fellow in there with a hundred head of chunky red and white cattle just to see if they could make it through the winter. The man came past here last month. Said the cattle plumb froze to death. There's grass there, prettiest you ever saw, but that infernal cold . . .'

'Red and white cattle?' Meredith asked.

'White-faced. I never saw any like 'em before.'

Meredith had. Herefords. They didn't freeze easily.

'What did the man look like?'

The description could have fitted Jack Sarrett, an old sort of Sarrett who didn't laugh any more.

Meredith went into Zebulon Valley. The agent had been right about the cold, but where the sun had worked a little, on southern slopes above a river as crooked as bent striped candy, there was bare sage and forage.

He found the carcasses of fifteen steers, and studied them a long time before he was sure they had been shot instead of frozen to death. In another month no one could have said. It took him three days to find the herd hidden in a feeder valley where they could paw snow for forage. They weren't in bad shape, considering. They had two bulls with them, and there was a good calf crop about due.

Inch by inch Meredith searched the big aspen log cabin he found at the lower end of the valley. It was well stocked with food. It was crudely built, but it was tight. Somebody had spent a lot of time hacking out furniture with an Army-issue axe. He frowned a long time at the second bunk, a small one with a bottom of willows crudely woven. No child had ever used it, because the upraised edges of the drying bark were unbroken.

Just another blind lead, Meredith thought. It was just one of many he'd followed. He'd been right about someone's pulling a sandy on the government. The man had shot a few steers as evidence to back up his report about the herd freezing. In a few weeks he could begin to move them deeper into the mountains, or just leave them where they were.

Any government official stupid enough to wonder if Herefords would freeze in this country wouldn't know enough to investigate thoroughly. And to a man who didn't know much, the scattered bones of fifteen steers

45

would look like any number.

The whole thing smelled like a Sarrett trick, but it was too small, involving too much work. And that little bunk ... no, he'd followed a bad hunch. He'd rest here overnight and be on his way in the morning.

Soon after the heat of the tiny cookstove hit him he was terribly drowsy. He went out and took care of Buzzer. There was nothing to do but turn him loose and let him forage with the cattle.

Meredith didn't eat himself. He stoked the fire and lay down on the big bunk, with his gun under the sheepskin coat he was using as a pillow. These failures were coming to hit him harder and harder, now that there was special urgency to finish Sarrett before he spoiled Mary's life.

The picture started years ago at Andy McRae's corral in the *brasada* was grooved deeply in Meredith's brain: finding Jack Sarrett, calling to him, watching him turn. Then he'd remind Sarrett of why he was going to die. The rest was a beautiful explosion of savagery, a vision so clear that it had brought Meredith from sleep many times, his teeth gritted, his hand holding a smoking, bucking gun so real that he'd had to look hard to know it was not there.

He was sound asleep in the heat when someone kicked open the door and walked in.

Meredith had his gun and was off the bunk

46

before he knew more than that a man was in the room.

Blinding snow glare was all around the man, so that Meredith could scarcely see his lower body. But the fellow's head was well above the top of the open door, where the glare from outside did not hide anything. His hat was dragged down tight over a ragged shawl that Jack Sarrett would not have used to wipe down a lathered horse. Frost was just starting to melt on an unkempt black beard.

But nothing could change the gray eyes and the set of the wide mouth.

There he stood, the man who had made Meredith's life a bitter, searching hell, the man who had laughed at him for years. A hundred triumphant, blazing words ran in Meredith's brain. He couldn't say them all at once.

'You're mine, you dirty son!' he finally said.

Sarrett just stood there with the cold-fog rolling around him from the open doorway. Meredith didn't have to see more than his face, for his gun knew where to send its churning lead.

'Remember me, Sarrett?'

'I knew you were here, Brett, when I saw the same old Mexican sorrel out there with the cattle. About nine years old now, ain't he?'

Smooth, Sarrett was, like always; ready to talk himself out of any crack. His hands would be stiff from cold. He wanted a little time. That was fine. That was the way Meredith had always seen it. Jack Sarrett would get an even chance.

'Pull that door shut with your foot!'

Sarrett hooked the door shut with his foot. The glare from outside was killed. Meredith could see all of him clearly now.

Sarrett was holding a child, wrapped to the eyes in gray blankets.

The sight raised an unreasoning, savage frenzy in Meredith. 'Put that brat down!' he yelled.

The boy that Sarrett unwrapped and stood on the dirt floor was pale and big-eyed, with a running nose and a face pinched from cold. He backed against Sarrett, staring at Meredith.

'Push him away!' Meredith said.

'Shall I kick him across the room?' The boy had clutched Sarrett's leg.

Cattle bawled uneasily in the little valley while Meredith stood staring at Sarrett. This wasn't the man he had followed so long. It wasn't the insolent, laughing Sarrett who had ridden away from Gypsum Hill.

But still his name was Jack Sarrett and he had to die.

'How do I get this kid back where he belongs?' Meredith asked.

'He belongs here.'

'You lie! Where's his folks? Where did you steal him?'

'His folks are dead,' Sarrett said.

The Indian agency where Meredith had left

his packhorse was only about thirty miles away. He could leave the kid there. 'Your fingers warm enough?' he asked.

'Good enough—if I had a gun.'

'You lie again! Unbutton that sheepskin.'

Sarrett had no gun.

Everything was wrong with the way he'd planned things to go. 'Your gun out there on your horse?'

'I've got a rifle behind the seat in the wagon.'

Wagon? Meredith had heard no wagon. He studied Sarrett narrowly. 'We'll get that gun,' he said.

The boy hung tight to Sarrett's hand as they walked through creaking snow to a spring wagon. It was going to be nasty for a kid, but when Sarrett tried his trick at the wagon . . .

He didn't. First, he lifted from the box a calf that had been bedded down in sawdust. It bawled and ran to its mother tied behind the wagon. After a while Sarrett shoved the calf aside and stole some of the milk in a bucket.

Still ready with his gun, Meredith took the rifle. It had been put away so carelessly that Sarrett couldn't have got it out in a hurry if he'd tried.

For the first time since Sarrett kicked the door open, Meredith wasn't quite sure of how to handle things.

They sat across the table from each other after the boy was asleep in the little bunk.

49

Sarrett rolled a cigarette slowly. His hands were work-marked, Meredith observed. He'd be slow when the showdown came, so Meredith would have to see that he got an even chance.

It had to be settled Meredith's way. He'd ridden too far too many years for it to be any other way.

When the cigarette was going, Sarrett said, 'I ran out on you down there at Elfego's place, sure. You weren't the first or last, but it's all done now.'

'Almost.' Meredith nodded. 'Let's hear your side—if you think you've got one.'

'No side to it,' Sarrett said. 'But I'll tell you.'

The far valleys and towns flowed down his voice. The facts were all in and Sarrett denied none of them. He made some of them more damning. But from the first, Meredith sat looking at a man who didn't fit the past as it had been.

' . . . Sure, I laughed about it all, and after you got on my tail and I found it out, I had more laughs from that than anything. It was great—until I met a girl in Larned, Kansas.' He looked up from under his brows. The candle was on a shelf above them, where Meredith had put it so that it could not be knocked out quickly. It put deep hollows into Sarrett's face.

'I know, you've heard that one before, Brett. After you dropped a horn for me you probably never looked seriously at any woman. You could always take 'em or ride on by, and so could I—until this happened.'

Creaking cold put its weight against the cabin. The boy in the bunk breathed softly.

'She wasn't pretty,' Sarrett said, 'but there was something in her eyes and the way she smiled—'

'Skip that part!'

'All right. She wouldn't marry me, and I know now, and should have known at the time, that it was a good thing she wouldn't—for her, at least. But I'll take an oath that I was honest and sincere at the time.'

'Oh, sure!' Meredith said.

Sarrett stared at the table. 'You know how it is when you've rolled out after the best night's sleep you ever had, and while you're taking your first drag on a smoke you look out on a range that's just been washed shining clean by rain, with the sky so clear it hurts to look at it—and you're not thinking about yourself at all, or any stunts you want to pull. For just a little while everything is like it ought to be with a man.' Sarrett nodded to himself.

'That's the way it was when I looked at Mary Linford.'

'Damn you, I said to skip that stuff!' Mary's face was so clear that all Meredith's old hurt and bitterness came back. He saw Sarrett give him a quick, odd glance.

'I don't say she changed me,' Sarrett said. 'I

tried to change some and maybe I did—for a while. I know my thinking changed some.' Shadows from outside and inside lay strong on his face. 'She was in love with a townsman, a two-by-four kid that had never been out in the rain. She finally made me believe it.

'I rode away, and I wasn't much good for a while. I pulled a few jobs and didn't get any kick out of them. The money went like it always did—with less pleasure. I started back to see old Andy McRae in Texas, and that was a bad mistake. The Rangers got me cold. A bullet through the chest, three years in a cell. I won't say that I thought about my sins much, because all I thought about was busting out of there.

'When they let me go, I wasn't exactly the same man that went in, not that I wasn't glad enough to get out. I spent a week with Andy. They come and go at his place, so he knew you'd been after me.' Sarrett looked up quickly. 'He got the money you sent, Brett. Andy said to look you up and make peace. Believe me, or go to hell—that's what I started out to do when I left there.'

'To hell with you.'

'I stopped in Larned to see Mary. She was married, of course, and gone. I found her in Denver. Her husband had sunk his money in a mine that was nothing, then he'd blown what little she had from her father. He couldn't stand being broke, and she was a drag to him then, so he skipped out and went back to the hills.'

Meredith clamped his jaw hard to keep from yelling a curse.

Sarrett's eyes were cloudy in the shadow-jumpy light. 'She was working in a dancehall, Brett, one a little worse than most. It was the dirtiest jolt I've ever had to take to see her there. She wouldn't leave. I couldn't force her out. I offered her money and she said no. I didn't have it, but if she'd said yes I'd have got it quick. She said she was going to save her money and hunt her husband up. He'd just had a little hard luck, she said.'

Meredith leaned forward, his jaw muscles quivering, his face as stiff as brittle leather.

'I went looking for that husband, Brett. I told him where she was and his townsman's scruples stuck out all over him in a second. All he could ask was why didn't she go back to her father. I knocked him clear across a room, and then I pulled my gun to kill him. I put it on him and between me and that gun Mary's face came up as clear as I see yours now.

'When I got back to Denver, Mary was dead of pneumonia.'

'Dead?'

Sarrett nodded, his eyes haunted and old. 'Her boy had been left in an old shack with a drunken woman to take care of him.'

Meredith's head jerked toward the little bunk.

Sarrett nodded. 'That's him. I had him with some decent folks there, but this spring I knew they were going back east. I want him, Brett. His father has lost all right to him, and his grandfather is too old to do much for him.'

Meredith rose. 'I'm going to kill Roger Hammond.'

Sarrett stared at him. 'I'd begun to guess that you'd loved Mary too.'

'I'm going to kill Hammond.'

'Sit down, Brett. We still have our problem.'

Meredith sat down slowly. That was so. No matter what, this man was still Jack Sarrett. It was hard now to believe that he was, but he was.

'This is going to be the greatest ranching country in the state someday,' Sarrett said. 'My idea was to steal that herd and make a start for the boy. It's no good that way. When I went to Denver I only lied a little—about the fifteen steers I shot. All right, there's no herd, but the country's still here, and I've seen it in summer. One of us is going to hold down everything I've filed on and make a spread for that boy someday.'

Meredith licked his lips. He had no anger left against Jack Sarrett, and he couldn't figure where it had gone, but still the thought that had driven him was grooved in his brain, without a will.

'I traded my gun for that wagon,' Sarrett said. 'But you always carried a spare gun in your blanket roll. The moon ought to be up now. It'll be bright as day out there on the snow. We'll go far enough from the cabin so we don't scare the boy. When he wakes up in the morning—the one who isn't here just rode away in the night, understand?'

Sarrett shook his head slowly. 'It isn't my way, Brett, and I know you think I'm trying to run something past you with talk. I told you when I left McRae's it was with the idea of making peace if you wanted it. You don't want it, and that's all right with me. I never did back down to any man and I'm not starting now. If I tried to crawl, I wouldn't be fit to think I could have raised Mary's boy and given him the right ideas about things.'

Sarrett looked across the table steadily. A trace of his old smile flashed in the dark beard, a softer smile with the old mockery gone. 'Anytime you say the word, Brett.'

Meredith looked at the work-stiffened hands. He looked to where candlelight fell dimly on the sleeping boy.

Sarrett himself had gone a long way toward bringing decision. There were others though, and their words spoken far down the long trails of yesterday were just coming through to Meredith. Old Andy McRae, Pearl in the dirty room in Granada and Mary Linford, with her eyes and smile as clear and beautiful as the range Sarrett had described.

The gun in Meredith's hand was far heavier

55

now than it had been when he plunged and stumbled through the brush with fever swarming through him. He pushed it across the table.

Sarrett looked at it a moment. 'I remember when you bought that in Austin. Mine was just like it.' He pushed it back across the table.

Meredith picked it up and tossed it under the large bunk. He took off his hat, the fifth one that had carried the same small packet sewed inside.

'We got a hundred to start with,' he said. 'Two of us can do something with this country—and the boy.'

GREAT MEDICINE

Deep in the country of the Crows, Little Belly squatted in the alders, waiting for his scouts. The Crows were big and angry in the hills this summer, and there was time to think of that; but since Little Belly was a Blackfoot who had counted five coups he could not allow his fear, even to himself.

He waited in the dappled shadows for more important news than word of other Indians who did not love the Blackfeet.

Wild and long before him, the ridges whispered a soft, cool song. In shining steps beaver ponds dropped to the great river flowing east toward the land of those with the mighty medicine. Dark and motionless, Little Belly waited.

He saw at last brief movement on a far hill, a touch of sun on the neck of a pony, the merest flash of a rider who had come too close to the edge of the trees.

That was No Horns and his appaloosa. No Horns, as ever, was riding without care. He was a Piegan and Little Belly was a Blood, both Blackfeet; but Blackfeet loved no one, sometimes not even each other. So Little Belly fingered his English knife and thought how easily small things caused one to die.

He saw no more of No Horns until the scout

57

was quite close, and by then Whirlwind, the other scout, was also on the ridge. They came to Little Belly, not obliged to obey him, still doubtful of his mission.

Little Belly said to No Horns, 'From a great distance I saw you.'

'Let the Crows see me also.' No Horns stretched on the ground with a grunt. Soon his chest was covered with mosquitoes.

Whirlwind looked to the east. Where the river broke the fierce sweep of ridges there was a wide, grassy route that marked the going and coming of Crows to the plains. Whirlwind pointed. 'Two days.'

'How many come?' Little Belly asked.

Whirlwind signalled fifty. 'The Broken Face leads.'

No white man in the mountains was greater than the trapper chief, Broken Face. He took beaver from the country of the Blackfeet, and he killed Blackfeet. The Crows who put their arms about him in his camps thought long before trying to steal the horses of his company. If there was any weakness in Broken Face it was a weakness of mercy.

So considering, Little Belly formed the last part of his plan.

Half dozing in the deep shade where the mosquitoes whined their hunting songs, No Horns asked, 'What is this medicine you will steal from the white trappers?'

It was not muskets. The Blackfeet had killed

Crows with English guns long before other white men came from the east to the mountains. It was not ponies. The Blackfeet traded with the Nez Perces for better horses than any white trapper owned. It was not in the pouches of the white men, for Little Belly had ripped into the pouches carried on the belts of dead trappers, finding no great medicine.

But there was a power in white men that the Blackfeet feared. Twice now they had tried to wipe the trappers from the mountains forever, and twice the blood cost had been heavy; and the white men were still here. Little Belly felt a cold chill, born of the heavy shade and the long waiting, but coming mostly from the thought that what he must steal might be something that could not be carried in pouches.

He stood up. 'I do not know what it is, but I will know it when I see it.'

'It is their talk to the sky,' Whirlwind said. 'How can you steal that?'

'I will learn it.'

No Horns grunted. 'They will not let you hear.'

'I will travel with them, and I will hear it.'

'It is their Man Above,' Whirlwind said. 'He will know you are not a white man talking.'

'No,' Little Belly said. 'It is something they carry with them.'

'I did not find it,' No Horns said. 'And I

59

have killed three white men.'

'You did not kill them soon enough,' Little Belly said.

'If their medicine had been strong, I could not have killed them at all.' No Horns sat up. He left streaks of blood on the heavy muscles of his chest when he brushed mosquitoes away. 'Their medicine is in their sky talk.'

Whirlwind said, 'The Nez Perces sent chiefs to the white man's biggest town on the muddy river. They asked for a white man to teach them of the Man Above, so that they could be strong like the white men. There were promises from the one who went across these mountains long ago. The chiefs died. No white man came to teach the Nez Perces about the sky talk to make them strong.'

'The Nez Perces were fools,' Little Belly said. 'Does one go in peace asking for the ponies of the Crows? It is not the sky talk of the trappers that makes them strong. It is something else. I will find it and steal it.'

Whirlwind and No Horns followed him to the horses. Staying in the trees, they rode close to the place, close to a place where the trappers going to their summer meeting place must pass.

Little Belly took a Crow arrow from his quiver. He gave it to Whirlwind, and then Little Belly touched his own shoulder. Whirlwind understood but he hesitated.

He said, 'There are two days yet.'

'If the wound is fresh when the trappers come, they will wonder why no Crows are close,' Little Belly said.

No Horns grinned like a buffalo wolf, showing his dislike of Little Belly. He snatched the arrow from Whirlwind and fitted it to his bow and drove it with a solid chop into Little Belly's shoulder.

With his face set to hide his pain Little Belly turned his pony and rode into the rocks close by the grassy place to wait for the coming of the trappers. The feathered end of the shaft rose and fell to his motion, sawing the head against bone and muscle.

He did not try to pull the arrow free while his companions were close. When he heard them ride away on the long trip back to Blackfoot country he tried to wrench the arrow from his shoulder. The barbs were locked against bone. They ground on it. The pain made Little Belly weak and savage, bringing water to his face and arms.

He sat down in the rocks and hacked the tough shaft off a few inches from his shoulder. He clamped his teeth close to the bleeding flesh, trying with strong movements of his neck to draw the iron head. Like a dog stripping flesh from a bone he tugged. The arrow seemed to loosen, dragging flesh and sinew with it; but the pain was great. All at once the sky turned black.

Little Belly's pony pulled away from the

unconscious man and trotted to join the other two.

When Little Belly came back to the land of sky and grass he was willing to let the arrow stay where it was. It was better, too, that the white men would find him thus. But that night he was savage again with pain. He probed and twisted with the dull point of his knife until blood ran down and gathered in his breech clout. He could not get the arrow out. He thought then that he might die, and so he sang a death song, which meant that he was not afraid to die, and therefore, could not die.

He dozed. The night was long. It passed in time and the sun spread brightness on the land of the Crows. Hot and thirsty, Little Belly listened to the river, but he would not go to it in daylight. It was well he did not, for seven long-haired Crows came by when the sun was high. Three of them saw his pony tracks and came toward the rocks. Others, riding higher on the slope, found the tracks of all three horses. They called out excitedly.

A few seconds more and the two Crows coming toward Little Belly would have found him and chopped him up, but now they raced away to join the main hunt.

All day the wounded Blackfoot burned with thirst. The sun was hotter than he ever remembered before; it heaped coals on him and tortured his eyes with mist. When night came he waded into the tugging current of the

62

river, going deep, bathing his wound and drinking. By the time he had crept into the rocks again he was as hot as before. Many visions came to him that night but they ran so fast upon each other afterward he could not remember one of them clearly enough to make significance from it.

Old voices talked to him and old ghosts walked before him in the long black night. He was compressed by loneliness and the will to carry out his plan wavered. Sometimes he thought he would rise and run away, but he did not go.

From afar he heard the trappers the next day. He crawled to the edge of the rocks. The Delaware scouts found him, grim, incurious men who were not truly Indians but brothers of the white trappers. Little Belly hated them.

Without dismounting, they watched him, laughing. One of them tipped his rifle down.

Little Belly found strength to rise then, facing the Delawares without fear. The dark, ghost-ridden hours were gone. These were but men. All they could do to Little Belly was kill him. Little Belly looked at them and spat.

Now their rifles pointed at his chest, but when the Delawares saw they could not make him afraid, they dismounted and flung him on the ground. They took his weapons. They grunted over his strong Nez Perce shield, thumping it with their hands. Then they threw it into the river. They broke his arrows and threw away his bow. One of them kept his knife.

When they took his medicine pouch and scattered the contents on the ground, Little Belly would have fought them, and died, but he remembered that he had a mission.

The big white man who came galloping on a powerful horse was not Broken Face. This white man's beard grew only on his upper lip, like a long streak of sunset sky. His eyes were the color of deep ice upon a river. Strong and white his teeth flashed when he spoke to the Delawares. Little Belly saw at once that the Delawares stood in awe of this one, which was much to know.

The white man leaped from his horse. His rifle was strange, two barrels lying one upon the other.

'Blackfoot,' one of the Delawares said.

Curiously, the white man looked at Little Belly.

A Delaware took his tomahawk from his belt and leaned over the Blackfoot.

'No,' the white man said, without haste. He laughed. From his pocket he took a dark bone. A slender blade grew from it quickly. With this he cut the arrow from Little Belly's shoulder. He lifted Little Belly to his feet, looking deep into the Blackfoot's eyes.

Little Belly tried to hide his pain.

'Tough one,' the white man said.

The Delaware with the tomahawk spoke in

Blackfoot. 'We should kill him now.' He looked at the white man's face, and then reluctantly he put away his tomahawk.

Broken Face came then. Not far behind him were the mules packed with trade goods for the summer meeting. Long ago a Cheyenne lance had struck Broken Face in the corner of his mouth, crashing through below his ear. Now he never spoke directly before him but always to one side, half whispering. His eyes were the color of smoke from a lodge on a rainy day, wise from having seen many things in the mountains. He put tobacco in his mouth. He looked at Little Belly coldly.

'One of old Thunder's Bloods,' he said. 'Why didn't you let the Delawares have him, Stearns?'

'I intended to, until I saw how tough he was.'

'All Blackfeet are tough.' Broken Face spat.

Little Belly studied the two men. The Broken Face was wise and strong, and the Blackfeet had not killed him yet; but already there were signs that the weakness of mercy was stirring in his mind. It was said that Broken Face did not kill unless attacked. Looking into Stearns' pale eyes, Little Belly knew that he would kill any time.

'Couldn't you use him?' Stearns asked.

Broken Face shook his head.

Stearns held up the bloody stub of arrow. He smiled. 'No gratitude?'

'Hell!' Broken Face said. 'He'd pay you by slicing your liver. He's Blackfoot. Leave him to the Delawares.'

'What will they do?'

'Throw him on a fire, maybe. Kill him by inches. Cut the meat off his bones and throw the bones in the river. The Bloods did that to one of them last summer.' Broken Face walked to his horse.

'Couldn't you use him to get into Blackfoot country peacefully?' Stearns asked. 'Sort of a hostage?'

'No. Any way you try to use a Blackfoot he don't shine a-tall.' Broken Face got on his horse, studying the long ridges ahead. 'Likely one of the Crows that was with us put the arrow into him. Too bad they didn't do better. He's no good to us. Blackfeet don't make treaties, and if they did, they wouldn't hold to 'em. They just don't shine no way, Stearns. Come on.'

Not by the words, but by the darkening of the Delawares' eyes, Little Belly knew it was death. He thought of words to taunt the Delawares while they killed him; and then he remembered he had a mission. To die bravely was easy; but to steal powerful medicine was greatness.

Little Belly looked to Stearns for mercy. The white man had saved him from the Delawares, and had cut the arrow from his shoulder; but those two deeds must have been matters of curiosity only. There was no mercy in the white man's eyes now. In one quick instant Little Belly and Stearns saw the utter ruthlessness of each other's nature.

Stearns was greater than the Broken Face, Little Belly saw, for Stearns made no talk. He merely walked away.

The Delawares freed their knives. 'Is the Blackfoot a great runner?' one asked.

In his own tongue Little Belly spoke directly to Broken Face. 'I would travel with you to my home.'

'The Crows would not thank me.' Broken Face began to ride away, with Stearns beside him.

'Is the Blackfoot cold?' A Delaware began to kick apart a rotten log to build a fire.

'I am one,' Little Belly said. 'Give me back my knife and I will fight all of Broken Face's Indians! Among my people Broken Face would be treated so.'

'What did he say?' Stearns asked Yancey.

Yancey told him. He let his horse go a few more paces and then he stopped. For an instant an anger of indecision twisted the good side of Yancey's mouth. 'Let him go,' he said. 'Let him travel with us.'

The ring of Delawares was angry, but they obeyed.

It had been so close that Little Belly felt his limbs trembling; but it had worked: deep in Broken Face was softness that had grown since his early days in the mountains because he now loved beaver hides more than strength. Now he was a warrior with too many ponies.

Little Belly pushed between the Delawares and began to gather up the items from his medicine pouch. It shamed him, but if he did not do so, he thought they might suspect too much and guess the nature of his cunning.

Jarv Yancey—Broken Face—said to Stearns, 'You saved his hide in the first place. Now you can try to watch him while he's with us. It'll teach you something.'

Stearns grinned. 'I didn't know him from a Crow, until the Delawares told me. You know Blackfeet. Why'd you let him go?'

Broken Face's scowl showed that he was searching for an answer to satisfy himself. 'Someday the Blackfeet may catch me. If they give me a running chance, that's all I'll want. Maybe this will help me get it.'

'They'll break your legs with a club before they give you that running chance.' Stearns laughed.

There was startled shrewdness in the look the Mountain Man gave the greenhorn making his first trip to the mountains. 'You learn fast, Stearns.'

'The Scots are savages at heart, Yancey. They know another savage when they see him. Our wounded friend back there has a heart blacker than a beaten Macdonald trapped in a marsh. I took several glances to learn it, but I

68

saw it.'

The Delawares rode by at the trot, scattering to go on ahead and on the flanks as scouts. Neither Stearns nor Yancey looked back to see what was happening to Little Belly.

Ahead, the whispering blue of the mountains rose above the clear green of the ridges. There were parks and rushing rivers yet to cross, a world to ride forever. Behind, the mules with heavy packs, the *engagees* cursing duty, the wool-clad trappers riding with rifles aslant gave reason for Jarv Yancey's presence here. As Major Edmund Stearns looked through the sun-tangled air to long reaches of freshness, a joyous, challenging expression was his reason for being here.

Just for a while Yancey thought back to a time when he, too, looked with new eyes on a new world every morning; but now the ownership of goods, and the employment of trappers and flunkies gave caution to his looks ahead. And he had given refuge to a Blackfoot, which would be an insult to the friendly Crows, an error to be mended with gifts.

Stearns spoke lazily. 'When he said, "I am one," touched you, didn't it, Yancey? That's why you didn't let the Delawares have him.'

Jarv Yancey grunted.

*　　　*　　　*

The Blackfoot walked with hunger in his belly and a great weakness in his legs, but he walked. The horses of the trappers kicked dust upon him. The *engagees* cursed him, but he did not understand the words. He could not be humble, but he was patient.

And now he changed his plan. The Broken Face was not as great as the other white man who rode ahead, although the other was a stranger in the mountains. The cruel calmness of the second white man's eyes showed that he was protected by mighty medicine. Little Belly would steal greatness from him, instead of from Broken Face.

There would be time; it was far to the edge of Blackfoot country.

The one called Stearns took interest in Little Belly, learning from him some of the Blackfoot's history by talking slowly with the signs. Little Belly saw that it was the same interest Stearns had in plants that were strange to him, in birds, in the rocks of the land. It was good, for Little Belly was studying Stearns also.

It was Stearns who saw that Little Belly got a mule to ride. Also, because of Stearns, the Delawares quit stepping on Little Belly's healing shoulder and stopped their stripping of the blanket from him when they walked by his sleeping place at night.

There was much to pay the Delawares, and there was much to pay all the white men, too, but Little Belly held insults deep and drew within himself, living only to discover the medicine that made Stearns strong.

By long marches the trappers went closer to the mountains. One day the Crows who had ridden close to Little Belly when he lay in the rocks came excitedly into the camp at nooning, waving scalps. The scalps were those of No Horns and Whirlwind. Little Belly showed a blank face when the Crows taunted him with the trophies. They rode around him, shouting insults, until they had worked up rage to kill him.

The Broken Face spoke to them sharply, and their pride was wounded. They demanded why this ancient enemy of all their people rode with the friends of the Crows. They were howlers then, like old women, moaning of their hurts, telling of their love for Broken Face and all white trappers.

Broken Face must make the nooning longer then, to sit in council with the Crows. He told how this Blackfoot with him had once let him go in peace. The Crows did not understand, even if they believed. He said that Little Belly would speak to his people about letting Broken Face come into their lands to trap. The Crows did not understand, and it was certain they did not believe.

Then Broken Face gave presents. The Crows understood, demanding more presents.

Dark was the look the white trapper chief

71

gave Little Belly when the Crows at last rode away. But Stearns laughed and struck Broken Face upon the shoulder. Later, the Blackfoot heard the Delawares say that Stearns had said he would pay for the presents.

That was nothing, Little Belly knew; Stearns gave the Delawares small gifts, also, when they brought him plants or flowers he had not seen before, or birds they killed silently with arrows. It might be that Stearns was keeping Little Belly alive to learn about his medicine. The thought startled Little Belly.

Now the mountains were losing their blue haze. At nights the air was like a keen blade. Soon the last of the buffalo land would lie behind. There was a tightening of spirit. There were more guards at night, for the land of the Blackfeet was not far ahead. With pride Little Belly saw how the camp closed in upon itself by night because his people were not far away.

And still he did not know about the medicine.

Once he had thought it was hidden in a pouch from which Stearns took every day thin, glittering knives to cut the hair from his face, leaving only the heavy streak across his upper lip. On a broad piece of leather Stears sharpened the knives, and he was very careful with them.

But still he did not care who saw them or who saw how he used them; so it was not the knives, Little Belly decided. All day Stearns' gun was busy. He brought in more game than any of the hunters, and since he never made sky talk before a hunt, the Blackfoot became convinced that his powerful medicine was carried on his body.

At last Little Belly settled on a shining piece of metal which Stearns carried always in his pocket. It was like a ball that had been flattened. There were lids upon it, thin and gleaming, with talking signs marked on them. They opened like the wings of a bird.

On top of it was a small stem. Every night before he slept Stearns took the round metal from his pocket. With his fingers he twisted the small stem, looking solemn. His actions caused the flattened ball to talk with a slow grasshopper song. And then Stearns would look at the stars, and immediately push the lids down on the object and put it back into his pocket, where it was fastened by a tiny yellow rope of metal.

This medicine was never farther from Stearns' body than the shining rope that held it. He was very careful when the object lay in his hand. No man asked him what it was, but often when Stearns looked at his medicine, the trappers glanced at the sky.

Little Belly was almost satisfied; but still, he must be sure.

One of the *engagees* was a Frenchman who had worked for the English fathers west of Blackfoot country. Little Belly began to help him with the horses in the daytime. The Broken Face scowled at this, not caring for any kind of Indians near his horses. But the company was still in Crow country, and Little Belly hated Crows, and it was doubtful that the Blackfoot could steal the horses by himself, so Broken Face, watchful, let Little Belly help the Frenchman.

After a time Little Belly inquired carefully of the *engagee* about the metal ball that Stearns carried. The Frenchman named it, but the word was strange, so Little Belly soon forgot it. The *engagee* explained that the moon and stars and the sun and the day and night were all carried in the metal.

There were small arrows in the medicine. They moved and the medicine was alive, singing a tiny song. The *engagee* said one glance was all Stearns needed to know when the moon would rise, when the sun would set, when the day would become night and the night would turn to day.

These things Little Belly could tell without looking at a metal ball. Either the Frenchman was a liar or the object Stearns carried was worthless. Little Belly grew angry with himself, and desperate; perhaps Stearns' medicine was not in the silvery object after all.

All through the last of the buffalo lands bands of Crows came to the company, professing love for the Broken Face, asking why a Blackfoot traveled with him. The trapper chief gave them awls and bells and trinkets and small amounts of poor powder.

He complained to Stearns, 'That stinking Blood has cost me twenty dollars in goods, St. Louis!'

Stearns laughed. 'I'll stand it.'

'Why?'

'He wants to kill me. I'd like to know why. I've never seen a man who wanted so badly to kill me. It pleases me to have an enemy like that.'

Broken Face shook his head.

'Great friends and great enemies, Yancey. They make life worth living; and the enemies make it more interesting by far.'

The Mountain Man's gray eyes swept the wild land ahead. 'I agree on that last.' After a while he said, 'Besides wanting to kill you, which he would like to do to any white man, what does he want? There was three of them back there where the Delawares found him. He didn't have no cause to be left behind, not over one little arrow dabbed into him. He joined us, Stearns.'

'I don't know why, but I know what he wants now.' Stearns showed his teeth in a great streaking grin. 'I love an enemy that can hate all the way, Yancey.'

'If that makes you happy, you can have the whole damned Blackfoot nation to love, lock, stock and barrel.' After a time Yancey began to laugh at his own remark.

*   *   *

Little Belly was close to Stearns the evening
the grizzly bear disrupted the company, at a
bad time, when camp was being made. There
was a crashing on the hill where two *engagees*
were gathering wood. One of them shouted.
The other fired his rifle.

The coughing of an enraged bear came
loudly from the bushes. The *engagees* leaped
down the hill, throwing away their rifles. Little
Belly looked at Stearns. The big white man
was holding his medicine. He had only time to
snap the lids before grabbing his rifle from
where it leaned against a pack. The medicine
swung on its golden rope against his thigh as
he cocked his rifle.

Confusion ran ahead of the enormous silver
bear that charged the camp. The mules
wheeled away, kicking, dragging loosened
packs. The horses screamed and ran. Men fell
over the scattered gear, cursing and yelling as
they scrambled for their guns. There were
shots and some of them struck the bear
without effect.

Thundering low, terrible with power, the
grizzly came. Now only Stearns and Little
Belly stood in its path, and the Blackfoot was
without weapons. Little Belly fought with
terror but he stayed because Stearns stayed.
The white man's lips smiled but his eyes were

76

like the ice upon the winter mountains.

Wide on his feet he stood, with his rifle not all the way to his shoulder. Tall and strong he stood, as if to stop the great bear with his body. Little Belly put his hand over his mouth.

When Stearns fired the bear was so close Little Belly could see the surging of its muscles on the shoulder hump and the stains of berries on its muzzle. It did not stop at the sound of Stearns' rifle, but it was dead, for its legs fell under it, no longer driving. It slid almost to Stearns' feet, smearing the grass, jarring rocks.

For a moment there was silence. Stearns poured his laugh into the quiet, a huge deep laugh that was happy, wild and savage as the mountains. He looked at his medicine then, solemnly. He held it to his ear, and then he smiled and put it back into his pocket. He stooped to see how his bullet had torn into the bear's brain through the eye.

There was still confusion, for the mules and horses did not like the bear smell, but Stearns paid no attention. He looked at Little Belly standing there with nothing in his hands. Stearns did not say the Blackfoot was brave but his eyes said so. Once more he laughed, and then he turned to speak to Broken Face, who had been at the far end of camp when the bear came.

One of the *engagees* ran up and shot the bear in the neck. Broken Face knocked the man down for wasting powder and causing the animals more fright.

Quickly Little Belly left to help with the horses, hiding all his thoughts. Truly, this medicine of Stearns' was powerful. Little Belly could say that Stearns was brave, that he shot true, standing without fear, and laughing afterward. All this was true, but still there was the element of medicine which protected a brave warrior against all enemies.

Without it, bravery was not enough. Without it, the most courageous warrior might die from a shot not even aimed at him. In the round thing Stearns carried was trapped all movement of the days and nights and a guiding of the owner in war and hunting.

Now Little Belly was sure about the object, but as he pondered deep into the night, his sureness wore to caution. He could not remember whether Stearns listened to the talk of his medicine before the bear made sounds upon the hill or after the shouts and crashing began.

So Little Belly did not push his plan hard yet. He watched Stearns, wondering, waiting for more evidence. Sometimes the white man saw the hard brown eyes upon him as he moved about the camp, and when he did he showed his huge grin.

Three days from a vague boundary of ridges and rivers that marked the beginning of Blackfoot lands the Delaware scouts reported buffalo ahead. At once the camp was excited.

Broken Face looked at the hills around him, and would not let more than a few ride ahead to hunt.

Stearns borrowed a Sioux bow and arrows from one of the Delawares. He signalled to Little Belly. Riding beside Stearns, the Blackfoot went out to hunt. With them were the Delawares, Broken Face, and a few of the trappers. When Broken Face first saw the weapons Little Belly carried he spoke sharply to Stearns, who laughed.

Little Belly's mule was not for hunting buffalo, so the Blackfoot did not go with the others to the head of the valley where the animals were. He went, instead, to the lower end, where he would have a chance to get among the buffalo when the other hunters drove them. The plan was good. When the buffalo came streaming down the valley, the startled mule was caught among them and had to run with them, or be crushed.

In the excitement Little Belly forgot everything but that he was a hunter. He rode and shouted, driving his arrows through the lungs of fat cows. He could not guide his mount, for it was terror-stricken by the dust and noise and shock of huge brown bodies all around it. When there was a chance the mule ran straight up a hill and into the trees in spite of all that Little Belly could do to turn it.

He saw Stearns still riding, on through the valley and to a plain beyond where the buffalo still ran. Little Belly had one arrow left. He tried to ride after Stearns, but the mule did not like the valley and was stubborn about going into it. By the time the Blackfoot got steady movement from his mount, Stearns was coming back to where Broken Face and some of the other hunters were riding around a wounded bull that charged them in short rushes.

Down in the valley, Stearns said to Yancey, 'That bull has a dozen bullets in him!'

'He can take three dozen.' Yancey looked up the hill toward Little Belly. 'Your Blackfoot missed a good chance to light out.'

Stearns was more interested in the wounded buffalo at the moment. The hunters were having sport with it, running their horses at it. Occasionally a man put another shot into it. With purple blood streaming from its mouth and nostrils, rolling its woolly head, the bull defied them to kill it. Dust spouted from its sides when bullets struck. The buffalo bellowed, more in anger than in pain.

'How long can it last?' Stearns asked, amazed.

'A long time,' Yancey said. 'I've seen 'em walk away with a month's supply of good galena.'

'I can kill it in one minute.'

Yancey shook his head. 'Not even that gun of yours.'

'One shot.'

'Don't get off your horse, you damned fool!'

Stearns was already on the ground. 'One minute, Yancey.' He looked at his watch. He walked toward the bull.

Red-eyed, with lowered head, the buffalo watched him. It charged. Stearns fired one barrel. It was nothing. The bull came on. Stearns fired again. The buffalo went down, and, like the bear, it died almost at Stearns' feet.

'You damned fool!' Yancey said. 'You shot it head-on!'

Stearns laughed. 'Twice. For a flash, I didn't think that second one would do the work.'

Little Belly had seen. There was no doubt now: Stearns had made medicine with the round thing and it had given him power to do the impossible.

The hunters began to butcher cows. Fleet horses stood without riders. Little Belly had one arrow left, and Stearns was now apart from the others, examining the dead bull. But when the Blackfoot reached the valley Broken Face was once more near Stearns, with his rifle slanting toward Little Belly.

'Take that arrow he's got left,' Yancey said.

Stearns did so. 'I was going to give him his chance.'

'You don't give a Blackfoot any chance!' Yancey started away. 'There's other arrows sticking in some of the cows he shot. Remember that, Stearns.'

81

Little Belly did not understand the words, but the happy challenge of Stearns' smile was clear enough.

They went together to one of the cows Little Belly had killed. The white man cut the arrow from its lungs. He put the arrow on the ground and then he walked a few paces and laid his rifle on the grass. He looked at Little Belly, waiting.

The white man still had his medicine. It was too strong for Little Belly; but otherwise, he would not have been afraid to take the opportunity offered him. He tossed his bow toward the mule. The white man was disappointed.

They ate of the steaming-hot liver of the cow, looking at each other while they chewed.

That night the company of Broken Face feasted well, chewing dripping pieces of tender hump rib as they squatted at the fires. Little Belly ate with the rest, filling his belly, filling his mind with the last details of his plan.

When the stars were cold above he rose from his blanket and went to the fire. He roasted meat, looking toward the outer rim of darkness where Stearns slept near Broken Face. Then, without stealth, Little Belly went through the night to where the French *engagee* guarded one side of the horse corral.

The Frenchman saw him coming from the fire and was not alarmed. Little Belly held out the meat. The man took it with one hand, still holding to his rifle. After a time the guard squatted down, using both hands to hold the rib while he ate. Little Belly's hand trailed through the dark, touching the stock of the gun that leaned against the Frenchman's leg.

The *engagee* smacked his lips. The meat was still against his beard when Little Belly snatched the gun and swung it. Quite happy the Frenchman died, eating good fat cow. Little Belly took his knife at once. He crouched; listening. The rifle barrel had made sound. Moments later, the horses shifting inside their rope enclosure made sound also.

Little Belly started back to the fire, and then he saw that two trappers had risen and were roasting meat. He put the knife at the back of his belt and went forward boldly. He picked up his blanket and threw it around him. He lay down near Stearns and Broken Face.

One of the trappers said, 'Was that Blackfoot sleeping there before?'

Grease dripped from the other trapper's chin as he looked across the fire. 'Don't recall. I know I don't want him sleeping near me. I been uneasy ever since that Blood took up with us.'

After the white men had eaten they went back to their blankets. The camp became quiet. For a long time Little Belly watched the cold star-fires in the sky, and listened to the breathing of Stearns.

Then, silent as the shadows closing on the

dying fire, the Blackfoot moved. At last, on his knees beside Stearns, with the knife in one hand, Little Belly's fingers walked beneath the blanket until they touched and gripped the metal rope of Stearns' great medicine. To kill the owner before taking his medicine would mean the power of it would go with his spirit to another place.

Little Belly's fingers clutched the chain. The other hand swung the knife high.

Out of the dark came a great fist. It smashed against Little Belly's forehead. It flung him back upon the ground. The white stars flashed in his brain. He did not know then that he held the medicine in his hand.

Stearns was surging up. Broken Face was out of his blanket in an instant. The hammer of his rifle clicked. Little Belly rolled away, bumping into packs of trade goods. He leaped up and ran. A rifle gushed. The bullet sought him. He heard it tear a tree. He ran. The medicine bumped his wrist. Great was Little Belly's exultation.

Stearns' rifle boomed twice, the bullets growling close to Little Belly; but now nothing could harm him. The great medicine was in his hand, and his legs were fleet.

The camp roared. Above it all, Little Belly heard Stearns' mighty laugh. The white man had not yet discovered his terrible loss, Little Belly thought. Stearns and maybe others would follow him now, deep into the lands of his own people.

When day came Little Belly saw no sign that Stearns or any of the white men were pursuing him. It occurred to him that they were afraid to do so, now that he had stolen the power of the greatest of them.

The medicine was warm. All night he had carried it in his hand, sometimes listening with awe to the tiny talk it made. It frightened him to think of opening the lids, but he knew he must do so; this medicine that lived must look into his face and know who owned it now. He pried one lid open. There was another with a carved picture of a running horse and talking signs that curved like grass in the wind.

Now Little Belly knew why Stearns' horse had been more powerful and fleeter than any owned by other members of Broken Face's company.

Little Belly opened the second lid. His muscles jerked. He grunted. Golden talking signs looked at him from a white face. There were two long pointing arrows, and a tiny one that moved about a small circle. The song of the medicine was strong and steady, talking of the winds that blew across the mountains, telling of the stars that flowed in the summer sky, telling of the coming and going of the moon and sun.

Here was captured the power of strong deeds, held in the mysterious whispering of the medicine. Now Little Belly would be great forever among the Blackfeet, and his people would be great.

The age-old longing of all mankind to control events that marched against them was satisfied in Little Belly. He pushed the lids together. He held the medicine in both hands, looking at the sky.

In his pouch was his old medicine that sometimes failed, the dried eye of a mountain lion, a blue feather that had fallen in the forest when Little Belly saw no bird near, a bright green rock shaped like the head of a pony, the claw of an eagle, and other things.

Little Belly did not throw away the old medicine. It could help the new and make it even stronger.

*   *   *

When the sun was straight above the Crows were on his trail. He saw all three of them when they rode across a park. His first thought was to run hard, staying in the heavy timber where their ponies could not go. He had learned that on his first war party against the Crows long ago.

One of the enemies would stay on Little Belly's trail. The others would circle around to keep him from reaching the next ridge. It was a matter of running fast. Little Belly started. He stopped, remembering that he had powerful medicine.

86

He took it from his pouch and looked at it, as Stearns had done before he killed the bear, before he killed the great buffalo. The medicine made its steady whisper in the silent forest. It told Little Belly that he was greater than all enemies.

So he did not run. He went back on his own trail and hid behind a log. No jay warned of his presence. No squirrel shouted at him. His medicine kept them silent. And his medicine brought the Crow, leading his pony, straight to Little Belly.

While the Crow was turning, Little Belly was over the log with his knife. Quickly, savagely, he struck. A few minutes later he had a scalp, a heavy musket, another knife, and a pony. He gave fierce thanks to his medicine.

Little Belly rode into the open below one end of the ridge. The Crow circling there saw him and came to the edge of the trees. Little Belly knew him at once, Thunder Coming, a young war chief of the Crows. They taunted each other. Little Belly waved the fresh scalp. Thunder Coming rode into the open to meet his enemy. Out of rifleshot, they ran their ponies around each other, yelling more insults.

At last they rode toward each other. They both fired their rifles. They both missed. At once Thunder Coming turned his horse and rode away to reload.

Little Belly would have done the same, except that he knew how strong his medicine

87

was. He raced after Thunder Coming. The Crow was startled at this breach of custom, but when he realized that he was running from one who chased him, he swung his pony in a great circle to come back.

The Blackfoot knew what was in Thunder Coming's mind then. The Crow expected them to try to ride close to each other, striking coup, not to kill but to gain glory.

Little Belly let it begin in the old way but instead of striking lightly and flashing past, he crashed into Thunder Coming, and swung the musket like a war club.

Thunder Coming died because he believed in the customs of war between Blackfeet and Crows; but Little Belly knew he died because of medicine he could not stand against. There was food in Thunder Coming's pouch. That, along with his scalp, was welcome.

For a while Little Belly stayed in the open, waiting for the third Crow to appear. The last enemy did not come. Although the Blackfoot's medicine was great this day, he did not care to wait too long in Crow country. He went home with two Crow scalps and two Crow ponies.

The young men called him brave. The old chiefs were pleased. Little Belly boasted of his medicine. With it, he sang, the white men could be swept from the hills. The Blackfeet became excited, ready for battle. The women wailed because No Horns and Whirlwind were dead.

Each night when the first stars came Little Belly had talked to his medicine, just as he had seen Stearns do; but the Blackfoot did not let others see him when he twisted the small stalk that protruded from the flattened ball. The medicine made a tiny whirring noise to show that it was pleased.

While the Blackfeet made ready for war, sending scouts to report each day on the progress of Broken Face and his company, Little Belly guarded his medicine jealously. It was living medicine. It was what the white men would not reveal to the Nez Perces who had sent chiefs down the muddy river. Little Belly had not gone begging white men to tell what made them powerful; he had stolen the secret honorably.

Now he had the strength of a bear and the wisdom of a beaver. His fight against the Crows had proved how mighty was his medicine. With it he would be great, and the Blackfeet would be great because he could lead them to victory against all enemies.

It was right that he should begin by leading them against the trappers. Let the old chiefs sit upon a hill. Every day the scouts returned, telling how carefully the white men held their camps. The scouts named men they had seen in the company, strong warriors who had fought the Blackfeet before.

Thunder and the old chiefs were thoughtful. They agreed that it was right for Little Belly to lead the fight.

At last the Blackfeet rode to war.

*   *   *

For several days Jarv Yancey had been worried. The Delaware outriders were not holding far from the line of travel now; they had seen too much spying from the hills, and this was Blackfoot country.

'How do they usually come at you?' Stearns asked.

'When you're not looking for 'em,' Yancey said.

'Would they hit a company this big?'

'We'll find out.'

Stearns laughed. 'Maybe I'll get my watch back.'

'Be more concerned with holding onto your hair.'

The trappers camped that night in a clump of timber with open space all around it. Yancey sent the guards out into the open, and they lay there in the moonlight, peering across the wet grass, watching for movement from the black masses of the hills. The silence of the mountains rested hard upon them that night.

Cramped and wet, those who stood the late watch breathed easier when dawn came sliding from the sky and brought no stealthy rustling of the grass and shrieks and bullets.

All that day, the Delawares, on the flanks

and out ahead and on the backtrail, held closer and closer to the caravan. They knew; they smelled it. And Yancey and the other trappers could smell it too. Stearns was quieter than usual, but not subdued. His light blue eyes smiled into the fire that night before he went out to take his turn at guard.

The trappers watched him keenly. They knew how joyfully he risked his neck against big game, doing foolish things. The Bloods were something else.

Mandan Ingalls was satisfied. He said to Sam Williams, 'He don't scare for nothing. He's plumb anxious to tackle the Bloods. He'd rather fight than anything.'

'He come to the right country for it,' Williams said.

That night a nervous *engagee* fired his rifle at a shadow. Without shouting or confusion, the camp was up and ready in a moment. Then men cursed and went back to bed, waiting for the next disturbance. The old heads recalled the war cries of the Blackfeet, the ambushes of the past, and friends long dead. Remembering, the trappers slept well while they could.

*　　*　　*

When the moon was gone Little Belly led four young men in to stampede the white men's horses. They came out of a spit of timber and crawled to a winding stream. Close to the bank overhung with grass they floated down the creek as silently as drifting logs.

They rose above the bank and peered fiercely through the darkness. The smell of animals close by told Little Belly how well his medicine had directed him. A guard's rifle crashed before they were among the horses. After that there was no more shooting, for Broken Face himself was at the corral, shouting orders.

Besides the rope enclosure around the animals, they were tied together, and then picketed to logs buried in the earth. So while there was a great kicking and thumping and snorting, Little Belly and his companions were able to run away only the horses they cut loose.

But still, it was good. The raiders returned to the main war party with ten animals.

Remembering the uproar and stumbling about when the bear had charged the trappers as they prepared to rest, Little Belly set the attack for evening, when Broken Face would be making camp. Two hundred warriors were ready to follow the Blackfoot war chief.

The scouts watched the trappers. The Blackfoot moved with them, staying in the trees on the hills. A few young men tried to surprise the Delawares, but the white men's scouts were wary. In the afternoon Little Belly thought he knew where the trappers would stop, in an open place near a small stand of trees. They did not trust the dark timber, now that they knew the Blackfoot were watching.

Little Belly went to make his medicine.

He opened the lids to look upon the white face with the shining talking signs. Upon the mirror of the medicine was a drop of water, left from last night's swimming in the creek. Little Belly blew it away. His face was close to the medicine. The tiny arrow was not moving. Quickly, he put the round thing to his ear.

There was no whispering. The medicine had died.

Little Belly was frightened. He remembered how Stearns had laughed through the darkness when Little Belly was running away with the round thing. There was trickery in the medicine, for it had died as soon as Little Belly sought its strength to use against white men.

The Blackfoot let the medicine fall. It struck the earth with a solid thump. He stared at it, half expecting to see it run away. And then he saw the tiny arrow was moving again.

Little Belly knelt and held the round thing in his hands. It was alive once more. He heard the talking of the power inside, the power of white men who smiled when they fought. Once more that strength was his. Now he was warm again and his courage was sound.

Even as he watched, the arrow died.

In desperation, with all the memories of Blackfoot sorrows running in his mind, Little Belly tried to make the medicine live. He

93

talked to it by twisting the stalk. For a time the medicine was happy. It sang. The tiny arrow moved. But it died soon afterward. Little Belly twisted the stalk until the round thing choked, and the stalk would not turn any more.

He warmed the medicine, cupping it in his hands against his breast. Surely warmth would bring it back to life; but when he looked again there was no life.

He was savage then. This was white man's medicine, full of trickery and deceit. Little Belly hurled it away.

He went back to the Blackfoot warriors, who watched him with sharp eyes. Wind Eater said, 'We are ready.'

Staring through a haze of hate and fear, Little Belly looked below and saw Stearns riding with the lead scouts. 'It is not time yet.' The spirit of the medicine had fled back to Stearns.

'We are ready,' Wind Eater said.

Little Belly went away to make medicine, this time with the items in his pouch. He did many things. He burned a pinch of tobacco. It made a curl of white smoke in the shape of death.

Yesterday, it would have been death for Blackfoot enemies. Now, Little Belly could not read his medicine and be sure. After a while he went back to the others again. They were restless.

'The white men will camp soon.'

'Is not Little Belly's medicine strong?'

'The Broken Face will not be caught easily once he is camped.'

'Is not Little Belly's medicine good?' Wind Eater asked.

'It is strong,' Little Belly boasted, and they believed him. But his words struck from an emptiness inside. It seemed that he had thrown away his strength with the round thing. In desperation he considered going back to look for it. Maybe it had changed and was talking once more.

'We wait,' Wind Eater said. 'If Little Belly does not wish to lead us—'

'We go,' Little Belly said.

He led the warriors down the hill.

The length of Little Belly's waiting on the hill while dark doubts chilled him was the margin by which the Blackfoot surge missed catching the trappers as the bear had caught them. Little Belly saw that it was so. The thought gave fury to his movement, and if everyone had followed where he rode, the Blackfeet could have overrun the camp in one burst.

They knocked the Delawares back upon the main company. Straight at the camp the Blackfoot thundered, shrieking, firing muskets and arrows. The first shock of surprise was their advantage. The *engagees* leaped into the timber, forgetting all else. The trappers fired. While they were reloading Little Belly urged his followers to carry over them.

He himself got into the camp and fired his musket into the bearded face of a trapper standing behind a mule to reload his rifle. But there was no Blackfoot then at Little Belly's back. All the rest had swerved and were screaming past the camp.

Little Belly had to run away, and he carried the picture of Stearns, who had stood and watched him without firing his two-barrelled rifle when he might have.

The Broken Face gave orders. His men ran the mules and horses into the little stand of trees. They piled packs to lie behind. Broken Face rallied the *engagees*.

It was a fort the Blackfeet tried to ride close to the second time. The rifles of the trappers slammed warriors from the backs of racing ponies.

There would never be a rush directly into the trees, and Little Belly knew it. The fight might last for days now, but in the end, the white men, who could look calmly on the faces of their dead and still keep fighting, would win. They would not lose interest. The power of their medicine would keep them as dangerous four days from now as they were at the moment.

The Blackfeet were not unhappy. They had seen two dead white men carried into the trees. There were four dead warriors; but the rest could ride around the trees for a long time, shooting, yelling, killing a few more trappers. And when the Indians tired and went away, it would take them some time to remember that they had not won.

All this Little Belly realized, and he was not happy. True, his medicine had saved him from harm even when he was among the mules and packs; but if the white man's medicine had not betrayed him before the fight, then all the other warriors would have followed close upon him and the battle would now be over.

He rode out and stopped all the young men who were racing around the trees, just out of rifleshot. He made them return to the main body of warriors.

'I will kill the Broken Face,' Little Belly said.

Wind Eater smiled. 'By night?'

'Now. When it is done the others will be frightened with no one to lead them. They will be caught among the trees and we will kill them all.' His words were not quite true, Little Belly realized. The men who rode with Broken Face would not fall apart over his death, but an individual victory would prove how strong the Blackfeet were; and then they might go all the way in, as Little Belly had fought Thunder Coming, the Crow war chief.

Cold-seated in Little Belly's reason was the knowledge that one determined charge into the trees would end everything; but a voice whispered, *If the medicine is good.*

Signalling peace, Little Belly rode alone toward the trees. The Broken Face came alone to meet him.

'Before the sun dies I will fight Broken Face here.' Little Belly made a sweeping motion with his hand. He saw blood on the sleeve of the white man's shirt, but Broken Face held the arm as if it were not wounded. Little Belly knew that fear had never lived behind the maimed features of the man who watched him coldly.

'When you are dead the Blackfeet will go away?' Broken Face asked.

'If the white men go away when you are dead.'

Broken Face's mouth was solemn but a smile touched his eyes briefly. 'There will be a fight between us.' He went back to the trees.

When Stearns knew what had been said, he grinned. 'High diplomacy with no truth involved.'

'That's right,' Yancey said. 'But killing Little Belly will take a heap of steam out of the rest.'

'If you can do it.'

Yancey was surprised. 'I intend to.'

'Your arm is hurt. Let me fight him,' Stearns said.

Yancey bent his arm. The heavy muscles had been torn by a hunting arrow, but that was not enough to stop him. He looked at his packs, at mules and horses that would be fewer when the Bloods swept past again. Something in him dragged at the thought of going out. It was foolish; it was not sound business.

Casually he looked at his trappers. No matter what he did, they would not doubt his guts. Jarv Yancey's courage was a legend in the mountains and needed no proving against a miserable riled-up Blackfoot war chief. The decision balanced delicately in Yancey's mind. A man died with his partner, if the time came; and a man in command fought for those he hired, or he should not hire good men.

Yancey shook his head. 'I'll do it.'

'I thought so.' Stearns put his arm across Yancey's shoulder in friendly fashion, and then he drove his right fist up with a twist of his body. Yancey's hat flew off as his head snapped back. He was unconscious as Stearns lowered him to the ground.

'It's my fault that Little Belly is still alive,' Stearns said. He looked at Mandan Ingalls. 'You might take a look at Yancey's arm while things are quiet.'

Ingalls spat. 'For a while after he comes to, you're going to be lucky to be somewhere with only a Blood to pester you. If you don't handle that Blackfoot, Stearns, you'd just as well stay out there.'

Stearns laughed. He took his horse from the timber with a rush. Once in the open, looking at the solid rank of Blackfoot cavalry across the grass, he leaped down and adjusted his cinch. He waved his rifle at them, beckoning.

He vaulted into the saddle and waited.

The song of the dead medicine was in Little Belly's ears. It mocked him. Once more he had been tricked. Stearns, not Broken Face, was down there waiting. The power of the stolen medicine had gone through the air back to the man who owned it, and that was why the great one who laughed was waiting there, instead of Broken Face.

Silent were the ranks of Blackfeet and silent were the rifles of the trappers. Little Belly hesitated. The fierce eyes of his people turned toward him. In that instant Little Belly wondered how great he might have been without the drag of mystic thinking to temper his actions, for solid in him was a furious courage that could carry him at times without the blessing of strong medicine.

He sent his pony rushing across the grass. He knew Stearns would wait until he was very close, as he had waited for the bear, as he had faced the wounded buffalo. Riding until he estimated that moment at hand, Little Belly fired his musket.

He saw Stearns' head jerk back. He saw the streak of blood that became a running mass on the side of the white man's face. But Stearns did not tumble from his horse. He shook his head like a cornered buffalo. He raised the rifle.

Stearns shot the pony under Little Belly. The Blackfoot felt it going down in full stride.

He leaped, rolling over and over in the grass, coming to his feet unharmed. The empty musket was gone then. Little Belly had only his knife.

There was a second voice to the white man's rifle. The silent mouth of it looked down at Little Belly, but the rifle did not speak. Stearns thrust it into the saddle scabbard. He leaped from his horse and walked forward, drawing his own knife. The shining mass of blood ran down his cheek and to his neck. His lips made their thin smile and his eyes were like the ice upon the mountains.

It was then that Little Belly knew that nothing could kill the white man. It was then that Little Belly remembered that his own medicine had not been sure and strong. But still the Blackfoot tried. The two men came together with a shock, striking with the knives, trying with their free hands to seize the other's wrist.

Great was Stearns' strength. When he dropped his knife and grabbed Little Belly's arm with both hands, the Blackfoot could do nothing but twist and strain. The white man bent the arm. He shifted his weight suddenly, throwing his body against Little Belly, who went spinning on the ground with the knife gone from his hand and his shoulder nearly wrenched from its socket.

A roar came from the trees. The Blackfeet were silent. Stearns picked up Little Belly's knife.

Then, like the passing of a cloud, the cold deadliness was gone from Stearns. He held the knife, and Little Belly was sitting on the ground with one arm useless; but the white man did not know what to do with the knife. He threw it away suddenly. He reached out his hand, as if to draw Little Belly to his feet.

The trappers roared angrily. Stearns drew his hand back. Little Belly was no wounded buffalo, no charging bear; there was no danger in him now. Stearns did not know what to do with him. Seeing this, the Blackfoot knew that the greatest of white men were weak with mercy; but their medicine was so strong that their weakness was also strength.

Stearns went back to his horse.

'Shoot the stinking Blood!' a trapper yelled.

Stearns did nothing at all for a moment after he got on his horse. He had forgotten Little Belly. Then a joyful light came to the white man's eyes. He laughed. The white teeth gleamed under the streak of red beard. He drew his rifle and held it high. Straight at the Blackfeet ranks he charged.

For an instant the Bloods were astounded; and then they shouted savagely. Their ponies came sweeping across the trampled grass. Stearns shot the foremost rider. Then the white man spun his horse and went flying back toward the trees, laughing all the way.

Wild with anger, the Blackfeet followed too

far.

They raced past Little Belly and on against the rifle-fire coming from the island of trees. But too many Blackfeet rolled from their ponies. The charge broke at the very instant it should have been pressed all the way.

Little Belly saw this clearly. He knew that if he had been leading there would have been no difference.

His people were brave. They took their dead and wounded with them when they rode away from the steady fire of the trappers' rifles. They were brave, but they had wavered, and they had lost just when they should have won.

For one deep, clear moment Little Belly knew that medicine was nothing; but when he was running away with the rest of the warriors old heritage asserted itself: medicine was all. If the power of Stearns' round object, which could not be stolen for use against white men, had not turned Little Belly's bullet just enough to cause it to strike Stearns' cheek instead of his brain, the fight would have been much different.

Little Belly knew a great deal about white men now. They laughed because their medicine was so strong, so powerful they could spare a fallen enemy. But he would never be able to make his people understand because they would remember Little Belly was the one who had been spared.

As he ran from the field he knew it would have been better for him if Stearns had not been strong with mercy.

BIG GHOST BASIN

Young Bill Orahood, the Sky Hook owner, was waiting for Ken Baylor where the trail forked near the fall-dry bed of Little Teton Creek. Orahood was mostly arms and legs and a long neck. Without a word he swung his chunky sorrel in beside Baylor's horse and they rode toward Crowheart.

They went a quarter of a mile before Orahood blurted out the question that everyone was asking: 'What do you suppose got Paxton?'

Baylor shook his head. Maybe Doc Raven knew by now. Raven had not been in town late yesterday when a drifting rider brought Bill Paxton's body out of Big Ghost Basin.

'You saw Paxton?' Orahood asked. 'After—'

'Yeah.' It was something to forget, if a man could.

A mile from town they caught up with big Arn Kullhem. A wide chunk of a man, his flat jaw bristling with sandy stubble, Kullhem looked at them from deep-set eyes and did not even grunt when they spoke. His Double K lay right on the break into Big Ghost. More than any rancher, he had suffered from what was happening down in the basin.

Bridle bits and saddle leather and hooves against the autumn-crisp grass made the only sounds around them until they came to the top of the last rolling hill above Crowheart. Then Kullhem said, 'Doc Raven didn't give us no help on them first two.'

Bill Paxton was the third man to die in Big Ghost. First, an unknown rider, and then Perry Franks, Kullhem's foreman. Both Franks and Paxton, one of the twins of Crow Tracks, had staked out in the basin to get a line on the shadowy men who were wrecking the Crowheart ranchers. If they had died from bullets, Baylor thought, the situation would be clear enough.

'Who's going to stay down in the basin now?' Kullhem growled.

Orahood and Baylor looked at each other. Strain had been building higher on Orahood's blistered face the closer they rode to town. He and Baylor glanced over their shoulders at the hazed ridges that marked the break above the gloomy forests of Big Ghost.

Up here the grass was good, but when the creeks ran low, cattle went over the break to the timber and the swamps in the basin—and then they disappeared. Big Ghost was an Indian reservation, without an Indian on it. Fearful spirits, the ghosts of mutilated dead from an ancient battle with Teton Sioux, walked the dark forests of the basin, the Shoshones said. Even bronco Indians stayed clear of Big Ghost.

The cowmen had no rights in the basin; they

had been warned repeatedly about trespassing on Indian land, but their cattle were unimpressed by governmental orders. That made the basin a wealthy raiding ground for rustlers from the west prairies, who came through the Wall in perfectly timed swoops.

For a time the Crowheart ranchers had checked the raids by leaving a man in Big Ghost as lookout. Franks, then Bill Paxton. Baylor knew there was not a man left up here who would volunteer to be the third lookout in Big Ghost—not unless Doc Raven could say what it was a man had to face down there.

They crossed Miller Creek, just west of town. A man on a long-legged blue roan was riding out to meet them. Baylor looked up the street at a small group of men in front of Raven's office, and then across the street at a larger group on the shaded porch of the Shoshone Saloon.

Kullhem spat. 'You still say, Baylor, that Baldray ain't behind all this hell?'

'I do.' Jim Baldray, the Englishman, owned the I.O.T. His range was fenced all along the break, with permanent camps where the wire winged out. Baldray had the money to keep his wire in place. I.O.T. stuff did not drift down into Big Ghost. There was nothing against the Englishman, Baylor thought, except a sort of jealous resentment that edged toward suspicion.

'You and your brother-in-law don't agree,

107

then,' Kullhem said harshly.

Pierce Paxton, the twin brother of the man now lying on Raven's table, was not Baylor's brother-in-law yet, but he would be in another month.

Hap Crosby met them at the lower end of the street. He was the oldest rancher in the country. Sweat was streaking down from his thick, gray sideburns. He looked at Baylor. 'Baldray's here. Pierce wants to question him—if Raven don't have the answer.'

All the Paxtons had been savagely impatient when anger was on them. Pierce, the last one, would ask questions, answer them himself, then go for his pistol. Baldray would be forced to kill him. Pistol work was the first custom of the country the Englishman had learned; and he had mastered it.

'All right, Hap.' Baylor looked up the street again. He saw it now. He should have seen it before: the tension there on the Shoshone porch was as tangible as the feel of the hot sun.

'Did Doc—has he—' Orahood asked.

'No, not yet,' Crosby said curtly. 'Baldray's drinking with that drifter who brought Bill Paxton in.'

'Does that mean anything?' Baylor asked evenly.

'I didn't say so, did I?' Crosby answered.

Four other ranchers were waiting with Pierce Paxton at the hitch rail in front of

Raven's office. Paxton did not look around. Sharp-featured, tense, his black hat pushed back on thick, brown, curly hair, he kept staring at the doorway of the Shoshone. He was wound up, dangerous. He was fixing to get himself buried with his brother that afternoon, Baylor thought.

Slowly, sullenly, Arn Kullhem said, 'By God, I think he's right.'

'How far would you go to back that?' Baylor asked. 'Across the street?'

Kullhem's deep-set eyes did not waver. 'I wonder sometimes just where you stand in this thing, Baylor.'

Old Crosby's features turned fighting-bleak and his voice rang hard with authority when he said, 'Shut up, the both of you! We got trouble enough.'

It was the slamming of Doc Raven's back door, and then the whining of his well sheave that broke the scene and gave both Baylor and Kullhem a chance to look away from each other.

The ranchers stood there in the hot strike of the sun, listening to the doctor washing his hands. Orahood's spittle clung to his lips, and a grayness began to underlay his blisters. A few of the loafers from the Shoshone porch started across the street.

Doc Raven came around the corner of his building, wiping his hands on his shirt. He was a brisk, little, gray-haired man who had come to the country to retire from medicine and study geology.

'Well?' Kullhem rumbled, even before Raven reached the group.

Raven shook his head. His eyes were quick, sharp; his skin thinly laid and pink, as if it never required shaving. 'He was smashed by at least a dozen blows, any one of which would have caused death. His clothing was literally knocked from him, not ripped off. I can't even guess what did it.'

The sweat on Crosby's cheeks had coursed down through dust and was hanging in little drops on the side of his jaw. 'Maybe a grizzly, Doc?'

Raven took a corncob pipe from his pocket. He nodded. 'A silver bear would have the power, yes. But there isn't so much as a puncture or a claw mark on Paxton.'

'No bear then,' Orahood muttered.

Raven scratched a match on the hitch rail. 'It's like those other two cases. I don't know what killed any of them.'

With one eye on Pierce Paxton, Baylor asked, 'Could it be he was thrown from a cliff first, then—'

'No,' Raven said. 'Those granite cliffs would have left rock particles ground into the clothes and flesh.'

Pierce Paxton had turned his head to watch the doctor. Now he started across the street. Baylor caught his arm and stopped him.

'No, Pierce. You're off on the wrong foot.'

Paxton's face was like a wedge. 'The hell! How much of *your* stuff was in Baldray's holding corral that time?'

Baylor said, 'You know his men had pushed that stuff out of the wire angle. There was a man on his way to Crow Tracks to tell you when you and Bill happened by the I.O.T.'

'That's right, Pierce,' Crosby said.

'Say it was, then.' Paxton's lips were thin against his teeth. 'I want to ask Baldray how it happens he can ride Big Ghost, camp out there whenever he pleases, and ride out again, but Franks and my brother—'

'I ride it, too,' Raven said.

Paxton backed a step away from Baylor. 'They know damned well, Doc, that you're just looking for rocks!'

'Who are *they*?' Kullhem asked.

'That's what I'm going to ask Baldray.' Paxton knocked Baylor's hand away and started across the street. One of the loafers had already scurried inside. Baylor walked beside Paxton, talking in a low voice. The words did no good, and then Baldray was standing in the doorway, squinting.

The I.O.T. owner was a long, lean man, without much chin. He wore no hat. His squint bunched little ridges of tanned flesh around his eyes and made him appear near-sighted, almost simple. The last two to make an error about that expression had been drifting toughs, who jeered Baldray as a foreigner until they finally got a fight out of him. It had lasted two shots, both Baldray's.

Baldray blinked rapidly. 'Not you also, Baylor?'

Paxton stopped, set himself. The Englishman stepped clear of the doorway.

'Baldray—' Paxton said.

Baylor's rope-scarred right hand hit Paxton under the ear. The blow landed him on his side in the dust. Crosby and Doc Raven came running.

'Give a hand here!' Raven said crisply. Two of them stepped out to help carry Paxton away.

'The hotel,' Crosby said. He looked back at Baylor. 'I can handle him now.'

Baldray smiled uncertainly. 'Come have a drink, men!'

Across the street, the little knot of ranchers stared silently. Then Kullhem swung up, and said something to the others in a low voice. Orahood was the last. Baylor went into the Shoshone.

The gloom of the big room reminded him of the silent, waiting forests of Big Ghost. He stood at the bar beside Baldray, who was half a head taller. Kreider, who had found Bill Paxton at the edge of the timber in Battleground Park, took his drink with him toward a table. A man in his middle twenties, Baylor guessed. The rough black beard made him appear older. Just a drifting rider?

Baldray poured the drinks. 'Hard business, Baylor, a moment ago. I would have been forced to shoot him.'

'Yeah.' Baylor took his drink.

'Raven found nothing?'

'Nothing—just like the two others. What do you make of it, Baldray?'

The Englishman's horsy face was thoughtful. He smoothed the silky strands of his pale hair. 'A beast. It *must* be an animal of some kind. As a young man in Africa I saw things you would not believe, Baylor; but I still contend there must have been credible explanations... And yet there are strange things that are never explained, and they leave you wondering forever.'

There was a hollow chord in Baldray's voice, and it left a chill on Baylor's spine when he thought of Big Ghost and of the way Bill Paxton had been smashed.

'The rustlers always did steal in and out of the basin, of course,' Baldray said. 'They nearly ruined me before I fenced the break and hired a big crew. You fellows made it nip-and-tuck by keeping a scout down there, but now with this thing getting your men...' Baldray poured another drink.

The 'thing' rammed hard at Baylor's mind.

'Isn't it sort of strange that this animal gets just our men, Baldray? After this last deal we won't be able to find a rider with guts enough to stay overnight in the basin. That means we'll be cleaned out properly.'

Baldray nodded. 'It does appear that this thing is working for the rustlers—or being used by them, perhaps. The solution, of course, is to have Big Ghost declared public domain.'

'Fifty years from now.'

'It's possible sooner, perhaps.' Baldray's face took on a deeper color. 'Fence. I'll lend what's needed for thirty miles. Damn it, Baylor, we're all neighbors!'

He had made the offer before and Kullhem had growled it down in ranchers' meeting. Fencing was not all the answer for the little owners. It was all right for I.O.T. because Baldray could afford a big crew, and because the cattle of other ranchers were drifting into the basin. Shut all the drifting over the break-off, and then the rustlers would be cutting wire by night. The smaller ranchers could not hire men enough to stop that practice.

Baylor looked glumly at his glass. The immediate answer to the problem was to go into Big Ghost and find out what was making it impossible to keep a lookout there. He walked across to Kreider.

'Would you ride down with me to where you found Bill Paxton?'

No man could simulate the unease that stirred on Kreider's dark face. 'You figure to come out before dark?'

'Why?'

114

'You could tell that this Paxton had been in his blankets when he got it. He shot his pistol empty before . . .' Kreider took his drink quickly. 'No, I don't guess I want to go down into the basin, even in daylight—not for a while.' He looked at Baldray. 'You don't run stuff down there, do you, Mr. Baldray?'

Baldray shook his head.

So the Englishman had hired this man, Baylor thought. There was nothing unusual about that, but yet it left an uneasy movement in Baylor's mind. 'You're afraid to go down there, huh?' he asked.

Kreider stared into space. 'Uh-huh,' he said. 'Right now I am.' He was still looking at something in his own mind when Baylor went out.

*   *   *

She was young, with red-gold hair and an eye-catching fullness in the right places. She could ride like a demon and sometimes she cursed like one. Ken Baylor looked at his sister across the supper table at Hitchrack, and then he slammed his fist hard against the wood.

'Sherry!' he said, 'I'll paddle your pants like Pop used to if you ever even think about riding down there again!'

'Can it. Your face might freeze like that.'

Baylor leaned back in his chair, glowering. After a few moments he asked, 'Where was

115

this moccasin track?'

'By a rotted log, just south of where Bill Paxton had camped.'

No Indian. Raven sometimes wore moccasins.

'There was a mound of earth where Bill's fire had been. Smoothed out.'

Kreider had mentioned the mound, but not the smoothness. 'At least, that puts a man into it,' Baylor said.

Sherry gave him a quick, narrow look. 'You felt it?'

'Felt what?'

'A feeling that something is waiting down there, that maybe those Shoshone yarns are not so silly after all.' She hurried on. 'Sure, I know whatever it is must be related in some way to the rustling, but just the same . . .'

After a long silence she spoke again. 'No one would go with you, huh?'

'Orahood. Just to prove that he wasn't scared.'

After he left Crowheart that morning Baylor had found the ranchers meeting at Kullhem's. If it had not been for Crosby, they would not have invited him to get down; and even then, desperate, on the edge of ruin, they had been suspicious, both of Baylor and each other.

'Old Hap Crosby wasn't afraid, was he?' Sherry asked.

'No. But he wasn't sure that getting this

thing would cure the rustling. He favored more pressure on the Territorial representatives to have Big Ghost thrown out as reservation land. Then we could camp down there in force.'

The others had ideas of their own, but threaded through all the talk had been the green rot of distrust—and fear of Big Ghost Basin. Baylor told Sherry about it.

'Damned idiots!' she said. 'In their hearts they know that Baldray—or no other rancher up here—is mixed in with the rustlers!'

Baylor hoped it was that way. He got up to help with the dishes, stalling to the last. They heard Gary Owen, one of Hitchrack's three hands, come in from riding the break.

'Take *him*,' Sherry said. 'He's not afraid of the devil himself.'

Baylor nodded.

'I'm going to Crowheart,' Sherry said. 'If Pierce still wants trouble with Baldray, it will start in town—except that I'll see it doesn't start.' She rode away a little later, calling back, 'So long, Bat-Ears. Be careful down there.'

Owen's brown face tightened when he heard the 'down there.' He was standing at the corral with Baylor. 'You headed into the Ghost?' he asked.

'Tonight.'

'Saw two men on the Snake Hip Trail today, a long ways off.' Owen removed his dun Scotch cap, replaced it. He lit a short-stemmed pipe.

'Want me to go along?' He forced it out.

Baylor tried to be casual. 'One man will do better, Gary.'

'Say so, and I'll go!'

Baylor shook his head. They could not smooth it out with talk.

Three times the ranchers had gone over the escarpment in daylight, ready for full-scale battle. On the second try they had found horse tracks leading away from cattle bunched for a drive through the West Wall. Crosby claimed the rustlers had a man in the basin at all times, watching the break. Baylor thought so, too. But the idea had been lost in the general distrust of each other after the third failure.

Baylor was not thinking of men as the neck of the dun sloped away from him on this night descent in the huge puddle of waiting blackness. The night and Big Ghost were working on him long before he reached the first stream in the basin.

He stopped, listening. The tiny fingers of elementary fear began to test for climbing holds along the crevices of Baylor's brain. He swung in the saddle, and when he put his pistol away he told himself that he was a fool.

Shroud moss hanging across the trail touched his face. He tore at it savagely in the instant before he gained control. He came from the trees into the first park. War Dance Creek was running on his right, sullenly, without splash or leap.

All the streams down here were like that. Imagination, Baylor argued. He had come over the break unseen. The moss proved he was the first one down the trail in some time. *The first rider, maybe. What is behind you now?* Before he could stop himself, he whirled so quickly he startled the dun.

Back there was blackness, utter quiet. He strained to see, and his imagination prodded him. There was cold sweat on his face. He cursed himself for cowardice.

Where the trail crossed the creek, he would turn into dense timber and stake out for the night. He was here, safe. There was nothing he could do tonight. In the morning . . .

It was night when the Thing got Paxton . . .

The dun's right forefoot made a sucking sound. The animal stumbled. There was no quick jar of the saddle under Baylor, and he knew, even as he kicked free and jumped, that the stumble had been nothing, that the horse had bent its knee to recover balance before he was clear of leather.

Baylor stood in the wet grass, shaken by the realization of how deeply wound with fear he was. The dun nosed him questioningly. He patted the trim, warm neck and mounted again. If there were anything behind him, the dun would be uneasy.

' . . . *there are strange things that will never be explained, Baylor* . . .' Baldray had said that in the Shoshone, and now Baylor was sure he had not been mocking him or trying to plant an idea.

Baylor spent the night sitting against a tree, with his blankets draped around him. The dun was tied on the other side of the tree. Baylor's carbine was close at hand, lying on the sheepskin of the saddle skirts. The carbine was too small of caliber, Baylor thought, too small for what he was looking for. What *was* he looking for?

Out of the dead silence, from the ancient, waiting forest, came another chilling question. *What is looking for you, Baylor?*

The night walked slowly, on cold feet. It passed at last. Baylor rose stiffly. He ate roast beef from his sack, and finished with a cold boiled potato. Raven was the only other man he knew who liked a cold spud. Raven had come to the Crowheart country just about the time cattle rustling began in earnest, after a long period of inactivity.

The nameless fears that had passed were now replaced with the suspicions of the conscious mind.

Early sunlight was killing dew when Baylor rode into Battleground Park. He picked up the tracks of Sherry's little mare, coming into the park from the Snake Hip Trail. Owen had seen two riders on the Snake Hip the day before, but there was no sign that they had come this far. He followed Sherry's trail straight to where Paxton had been killed.

Baylor studied the earth mound over the fire site. It was too smooth, and so was the torn garment around it; and yet, the earth scars still spoke of power and fury and compulsion. An ant hill made a bare spot in the grass not fifteen feet away. Paxton would have used that. Because of the nature of his business here he would have had it figured in advance.

Baylor picked up a tip cluster of pine needles. He stared at the spruces. Their lower branches were withered, but here was broken freshness from high above. He went slowly among the trees close to the fire site. Here and there Paxton had broken dead limbs for his fire, but there was no evidence that anything had come down from the high branches.

He tossed the tip cluster away and went south of the camp to the rich, brown mark of a rotted log. There were Sherry's tracks again, but no moccasin print.

Out in the grass the dun whirled uptrail. Baylor drew his pistol and stepped behind a tree. A little later, Baldray, wearing a fringed buckskin shirt, rode into the park with Doc Raven.

'We knew your horse,' Raven said. He was wearing Shoshone moccasins, Baylor observed.

Baldray's face turned bone-bleak when he saw a jumper fragment on a bush. 'Oh! This is the place, eh?' He swung down easily. 'Let's have a look, Raven.'

The doctor moved briskly. 'The devil!' he muttered. 'See how the fire has been covered.' His smooth, pink face was puzzled. He picked up the piece of jumper. 'Good Lord!'

Baldray's heel struck the tip cluster of pine needles and punched them into the soft earth. 'Did you discover anything, Baylor?'

'Nothing.' Baylor shook his head. Raven's saddlebags appeared to be already filled with rocks. Gary Owen said the doctor started at the escarpment and tried to haul half the country with him every time he went out. 'You fellows came down the Snake Hip?'

Raven was studying tree burls. 'We started in yesterday,' he said, 'but I had forgotten a manual I needed, so we rode out last evening.' He looked at Baldray. 'You know, James, in the big burn along the cliffs I've seen jackpine seeds completely embedded in the trunks. I have a theory—'

'Rocks, this time,' Baldray said. 'If you want to look at that quartz on the West Wall before night you'd better forget the tree seeds.' He blinked. 'Tree seeds? Now isn't that odd?'

When the two men rode west, Baylor stared at their backs, not knowing just what he thought.

Baylor spent the day working the edges of the swamps along lower War Dance. Cattle were wallowing everywhere. He was nagged by not knowing what he was looking for; he had expected to find some sign where Paxton had been killed, at least the moccasin track.

At sunset he came out in the big burn. Several years before, Indians had thrown firebrands from the cliffs to start a fire to drive game from the basin. The wind had veered, and the fire, instead of crowning across the basin, had roared along the cliffs in a mile-wide swath. That cured the Indians. Evil spirits, they said, had blown a mighty breath to change the wind.

With the bare cliffs at his back, Baylor looked across the spear points of the trees. The parks were green islands, the largest being Battleground Park, where Paxton had died. The Wall was far to his right, a red granite barrier that appeared impassable; but there were breaks in it, he knew, the holes where Crowheart cattle seeped away.

About a half-mile air-line a gray horse came to the edge of one of the emerald parks. Bill Paxton had ridden a gray into Big Ghost. Kreider had brought out only the rig.

Once down in the timber, it took an hour of steady searching before Baylor found the right park. The limping gray knee-high in grass was Paxton's horse, all right. It saw Baylor when he led the dun from the timber. It snorted and broke like a wild animal for cover. There was never a chance to catch it.

Baylor recoiled his rope, listening to the gray crashing away like a frightened elk. The horse had not been here long enough to go mustang. The terror of the night the Thing had got Bill Paxton was riding on the gray.

Night was coming now. Gloom was crouched among the trees. The little golden sounds of day were dead. *You are afraid*, Big Ghost said. *You will be like Paxton's horse if you stay here.*

Baylor went through a neck of timber between parks. In the dying light on lower War Dance he cut his own trail of the morning. Beside the dun's tracks, in the middle of a mud bar, he saw a round imprint. He hung low in the saddle to look. A man wearing moccasins had been on his trail. Here the man had leaped halfway across the mud bar, putting down only the toes and the ball of one foot to gain purchase for another jump to where the grass left no mark. The foot had slid a trifle forward when it struck, and so there was no way to estimate how large—or small—it had been.

Baylor was relieved. He could deal with a man, even one who used Indian tricks like that. If this fellow wanted to play hide-and-seek, Baylor would take him on—and catch him in the end, and find out why the man had erased the track that Sherry had seen.

Dog-tired, he made a cold camp far enough from War Dance so that the muttering water would not cover close sounds. He freed the dun to graze, ate a cold meal, and rolled up in his blankets. A wind ran through the timber.

Baylor rolled a smoke, and then he crumpled it. The scent of tobacco smoke would drift a long way to guide a man creeping in.

No man killed Paxton or the others.

Baylor lay wide awake, straining at the darkness, for a long time, until finally he slept from sheer exhaustion.

The morning sun was a wondrous friend. Baylor slopped the icy water of the stream against his face. The dun came from the wet grass and greeted him.

He rode south, then swung toward the Wall, crossing parks he had never seen before. He took it slowly, not watching his backtrail. In the middle of the day, after crossing a park just like a dozen others, he dismounted in the timber and crept back to make a test.

For an hour he waited behind a windfall. The first sound came, the breaking of a stick on the other side of the tiny green spot. Baylor had been half dozing by then. Too easy, he thought; something was wrong. He heard hooves on the needle mat.

He had expected a man on foot. He crawled away and ran back to the dun, placing one hand on its nose, ready for the gentle pressure that would prevent a whinny. A little later he heard sounds off to his left. The man was going around, sticking to the timber. Slowly Baylor led his horse to intercept the sounds. The other man came slowly also, and then

Baylor caught the movement of a sorrel, saw an outline of its rider.

He dropped the reins then and went in as quickly as he could. He made noise. The dun whinnied. The other rider hit the ground. A carbine blasted, funneling pulp from a tree ahead of Baylor. He shot toward the sound with his pistol. The sorrel reared, then bolted straight ahead.

It flashed across a relatively open spot. It was Pierce Paxton's stallion. 'Oh, God!' Baylor muttered. 'Pierce.'

'Pierce!' he yelled.

There was silence before the answer came. 'Baylor?' It was Pierce Paxton. He was unshaven, red-eyed.

He said, 'Who the hell did you think you were trying to take!'

Baylor put his pistol away. 'Moccasin Joe. Who were you shooting at?'

'Anybody that tried to close in on me like that!' Tenseness was still laid flat on Paxton's thin features. 'Who's Moccasin Joe?'

Baylor told everything he knew about the man.

Paxton shook his head, staring around him at the trees. 'It's not Raven. I've been watching him and Baldray from the time they went across Agate Park.'

'Why?'

Paxton stared. 'You know why.' He rubbed his hand across his eyes. 'I think maybe I was

126

wrong. We lost two men down here, Baylor, but Baldray and Raven never had any trouble. Now I know why. They got a cabin hidden in the rocks near the wall. They don't stay out in the open.' Paxton saw the quick suspicion on Baylor's face.

'Uh-huh, I thought so too, at first, Ken. I thought they knew what's loose down here, that they were hooked up with the rustlers. I watched them for a day and a half. All they did was pound quartz rock and laugh like two kids. They may be crazy, Baylor, but I don't think they're hooked up with the rustlers.'

Paxton rubbed his eyes again. 'Made a fool of myself the other day, didn't I? What did Sherry say?'

'Nothing much. We both made fools of ourselves a minute ago, Pierce . . . Let's catch your horse.'

The stallion had stopped in the next park west. Paxton went in and towed the horse back on the run. It saw the dun and tried to break over to start trouble. Paxton sawed down brutally on the bit before he got the horse quieted. That was not like Paxton. The nights down here had worked on his nerves, too.

They went back in the timber and sprawled out. Paxton lay with his hands over his face.

'How you fixed for grub?' Baylor asked.

'Ran out yesterday.' Paxton heard Baylor rustling in his gunny sack. 'I'm not hungry.' But he finally ate, and he kept looking sidewise at Baylor until he asked, 'You've been here two nights?'

'Yeah.'

'Any trouble?'

'Scared myself some,' Baylor said. 'Did you?'

'I didn't have to. Since the first night I spent here I've been jumping three feet every time a squirrel cut loose. I had a little fire on Hellion Creek that night, with a couple of hatfuls of wet sand, just in case.'

Paxton had started with a defensive edge to his voice, but now it was gone and his bloodshot eyes were tight. 'The stallion just naturally raised hell. He got snarled up on his picket rope and almost paunched himself on a snag. I got him out of that and then I doused the fire.

'From the way the horse moved and pointed, I knew something was prowling. It went all around the camp, and once I heard it brush a tree.'

The hackles on Baylor's neck were up.

'You know how a lion will do that,' Paxton said. He shook his head. 'No lion. The next morning in some fresh dirt where a squirrel had been digging under a tree, I saw a track'— Paxton put his hands side by side—'like that, Ken. No pads—just a big mess!' Paxton's hands were shaking.

'What was it, Baylor? The Thing that got Bill?'

The Thing. What else could a man call it? Baylor thought. He said, 'There's an explanation to everything.'

'Explain it then!'

'Take it easy, Pierce. We'll get it.'

The thought of action always helped steady Paxton. 'How?' he asked.

'First, we get this Moccasin Joe.' Baylor thought of something so clear he wondered how he had missed it. 'Did you stop in Battleground Park?'

'I didn't come down the Snake Hip.'

'Old Moccasin Joe has trailed me once, and now I think I know why.' The thought carried a little chill. 'Here's what we'll do, Paxton . . .'

Later, Baylor divided the food. It would be parched corn now, and jerky, about enough for two days, if a man did not care how hungry he got. 'Day after tomorrow,' Baylor said.

They rode away in different directions, Baylor going back to Battleground Park. He found the tip cluster that Baldray had stepped on, and dug it out of the earth and held it only a moment before dropping it again. Pine needles. Everything here was spruce. The fact had not registered the first time.

That tip cluster had come from a branch that Moccasin Joe had used to brush out sign. Probably he had carried the branch from across the creek. Moccasin Joe knew what the Thing was. He was covering up for it.

The dun whinnied. Baldray was riding into

the lower end of the park. He veered over when he saw Baylor's horse.

'You haven't moved!' Baldray grinned to show he was joking. He was clean-shaven. He appeared rested, calm. That came easier when a man slept in a cabin and ate his fill, Baylor thought.

'You look done in,' Baldray said.

'I'm all right.'

Baldray squinted at the fringes of his beaded shirt. His face began to redden. 'It's no good sleeping out. Bumps and things, you know. I have a cabin near the Wall. Built it four years ago. Raven's there now. I wish you'd use it, Baylor. I'll tell you how to find it.'

Paxton had taken care of that. 'I know,' Baylor said.

Baldray blinked. 'Oh!' He raised pale brows. 'Well, yes. I've been a little selfish. Reservation land, so-called. If the fact got around that someone had built here—'

Baylor picked up the tip cluster. 'What kind of tree is that from?'

Baldray squinted. 'Evergreen.'

'Spruce or pine?'

The Englishman laughed. 'You and Raven! I know evergreen from canoe birch, but that's about all.'

Baldray was one Englishman who had not run for home after the big die-ups of the no-chinook years. He should know pine needles from spruce; but maybe he did not.

Baldray's face was stone-serious when he asked, 'Any luck?'

Baylor shook his head.

'There are harsh thoughts about me.' Baldray's voice was crisp. 'Fifteen years here and I'm still not quite a resident, except with you and Crosby.' Baldray looked around the park. 'This won't be reservation always. Room for I.O.T. down here, as well as the rest—once the rustlers are dealt with, and the government sees the light.'

Baldray slouched in the saddle, rolling a cigarette. 'I have watched the breaks in the Wall from the rocks near my cabin. There is a sort of pattern to the way the scoundrels come and go. I would say, Baylor—it is a guess, but I would say—the next raid might be due to go out through Windy Trail.'

His smoke rolled and lit, Baldray started away. 'Windy Trail. I'm going to tell Crosby, some of the others. Good name, Crosby. English, you know.'

He rode away.

It was not entirely hunger that made Baylor's stomach tighten as he rode across the burn the next afternoon. Like the others, the night before had been a bad one, with his mind and the deep, still forests speaking to him. He did not know now whether or not he was being trailed, but he had played the game all the way, and if Paxton had done his part, things might come off as planned.

Paxton was there, crouched in the rocks near the east side of the burn. They exchanged clothes behind the jumble of fire-chipped stone.

'I went out,' Paxton said. 'Sherry wants to see you tomorrow morning in Battleground Park.'

'Why didn't you talk her out of it?'

'You know better.' Paxton was stuffing newspaper under the sweatband of Baylor's hat.

'What does she want?'

'I don't know. She told me to go to hell when I ordered her not to come down here. Then she rode over to I.O.T. to see Baldray. I left a note in the bunkhouse for Gary Owen to come here with her.'

They were dressed.

'Keep in plain sight on the burn,' Baylor said. 'And keep going.'

'All right.' Paxton took the reins. 'Kullhem found the rustlers on the west prairie two weeks ago.'

'Fine. Just right. Get going.'

He watched Paxton ride away, past the black snags and leaning trees. The dun had gone into the rocks and the dun had gone out a few minutes later, and the rider was dressed exactly as he had been when going in. It might work, if Moccasin Joe was still trailing with his little pine-branch broom. The dirty bastard.

The sun died behind the red Wall. A wind

came down across the rocks and stirred the tiny jackpines in the burn. Murk crept into basin.

The man came from sparse timber at the east edge of the burn. Buckskins. Probably moccasins. Long yellow hair under a slouch hat. He paused and looked up where the dun had disappeared two hours before.

Baylor watched from a crack between the rocks. The man came clear, lifting his body easily over fallen trees. He walked straight at the rocks, then swung a little to the uphill side. Baylor drew his pistol and took a position behind a rock where the man would likely pass.

The steps were close, just around the rock. They stopped. With his stomach sucked in, breathing through a wide-open mouth, Baylor waited to fit the next soft scrape to the man's position. Silence pinched at nerve ends before the fellow moved again.

In two driving steps Baylor went around the rock. He was just a fraction late, almost on top of a beard-matted face, two startled eyes and that tangle of yellow hair. He swung the pistol.

Moccasin Joe went back like a cat, clutching a knife in his belt. Baylor's blow missed. The pistol rang out on rock, and by then the knife was coming clear. Baylor drove in with his shoulder turned. The knife was coming down when the shoulder caught the man at the throat lacing of his shirt.

133

Baylor was on top when they went down. He got the knife arm then, and suddenly threw all his power into a side push. The man's hand went against the rock. Baylor began to grind it along the granite.

The rock was running red before Moccasin Joe dropped the knife. With the explosive strength of a deer, he arched his body, throwing Baylor sidewise against the rock. One of the man's knees doubled back like a trap spring, then the foot lashed out and knocked Baylor away.

Moccasin Joe leaped up. He did not run. He dived in. Baylor caught him with a heeled hand under the chin. The man's head snapped back but his weight came on. A knee struck Baylor in the groin.

Sick with the searing agony of it, Baylor grabbed the long hair with both hands. He kept swinging Moccasin Joe's head into the rock until there was no resistance but limp weight.

For several moments Baylor lay under the weight, grinding his teeth in pain; and then he pushed free, straightening up by degrees, stabbing his feet against the ground. The front sight of his pistol was smeared, the muzzle burred, and maybe the barrel was bent a little.

But he had the man who was going to tell him what was killing ranch scouts in Big Ghost Basin. Except for the knife, Moccasin Joe had carried no other weapon. Baylor cut the

134

fellow's belt and tied his hands behind him. Blood was smeared in the tangled yellow hair.

Baylor had never seen him before.

Going down the burn, the prisoner was wobbly, but he was walking steadily enough before they reached the park, where Paxton was to come soon after dark. It was almost dark now. Just inside the timber Baylor made Joe lie down, then tied his ankles with Paxton's belt.

Firelight was a blessed relief after black, cold nights. 'The first man killed here was one of yours, Joe,' Baylor said. 'You boys got on to something that makes it impossible for us to keep a man here. What is it?'

After a long silence Baylor removed one of his prisoner's moccasins. The man's eyes rolled as he stared at the fire. Baylor squatted by the flames, turning the knife slowly in the heat until the thin edge of the blade was showing dull red.

Where the hell was Pierce Paxton?

'Put out the fire,' Moccasin Joe said.

'Talk some more.' Baylor kept turning the blade. 'That first man was one of yours, wasn't he?'

'Yeah.' Moccasin Joe was beginning to sweat. The skin above his beard was turning dirty yellow.

Baylor lifted the knife to let him see it.

'Your Thing has got us stopped,' Baylor said. 'What is it?'

The firelight ran on a growing fear in the captive's eyes. He started to speak, and then he lay back.

'First, the flat of the blade against the bottom of your arch, then the point between the hock and the tendon. I'll reheat each time, of course.' Even to Baylor his own words seemed to carry conviction.

'Put the fire out!'

Baylor lifted the knife again. The blade was bright red. 'I saw Teton Sioux do this once,' he lied calmly.

Moccasin Joe's breath was coming hard.

'You covered up something where Paxton was killed, didn't you? And then you checked back and wiped out a track of your own that you had overlooked.'

'Yeah.'

'Keep talking.'

'I want a smoke. I won't tell you anything until I get a smoke!'

Baylor stared at the tangled face, at the terror in the man's eyes. For a customer as tough as this one had proved up in the rocks, he was softening pretty fast under a torture bluff.

Baylor laid the knife where the blade would stay hot. He rolled two smokes and lit them. He put one in Moccasin Joe's mouth.

'You got to untie my hands.'

'You can smoke without that.'

The cigarette stuck to the captive's lips. He

136

tried to roll it free and it fell into his beard. He jerked his head back and the smoke fell on the ground. Baylor put it back in the man's mouth. He untied the fellow's hands.

Moccasin Joe sat up and puffed his cigarette, rolling his shoulders.

'Let's have it,' Baylor said.

'The bunch that's been raiding here ain't the one from the west prairie, like you think. We been hanging out on the regular reservation. The agent is getting his cut.'

It sounded like a quickly made-up lie. 'Is Kreider one of the bunch?'

The captive hesitated. 'Sure.'

'Describe him.'

Moccasin Joe did that well enough.

'What killed Paxton?'

'Which one was he?'

'The last one—in Battleground Park.'

'I'll tell you.' Moccasin Joe made sucking sounds, trying to get smoke from a dead cigarette.

Baylor took a twig from the fire. He leaned down. The captive's hands came up from his lap like springs. They clamped behind Baylor's neck and jerked. At the same time Moccasin Joe ducked his own head. Baylor came within an ace of getting his face smashed against hard bone.

He spread his hands between his face and the battering block just in time. Even so, he felt his nose crunch, and it seemed that every

137

tooth in his mouth was loosened. He was in a crouch then, and Moccasin Joe's thumbs were digging at his throat. Baylor drove his right knee straight ahead.

Moccasin Joe's hands loosened. He fell back without a sound. Baylor stood there rubbing his knee. He could not stand on the leg for a while. The sensitive ligaments above the cap had struck squarely on the point of Moccasin Joe's jaw.

Once more Baylor cinched the man's arms tight behind his back. Let him die for want of a smoke. Blood dripped into the fire as Baylor put on more wood. He stared at the red hot knife, wishing for just an instant that he was callous enough to use it.

Where in hell is Paxton? he thought.

Blood began to stream down his lips. He felt his way to the creek and washed his face and dipped cold water down the back of his neck. After a while the bleeding stopped. Both sides of his nose were swollen so tight he could not breathe through them. His lips were cut.

I'm lucky, he told himself, getting out with only a busted nose after falling for an old gag like that.

You're not out of it yet, Baylor. It's night again.

Once more the old voices of Big Ghost were running in his mind. Baylor dipped Paxton's hat full of water and went back to the fire and Moccasin Joe.

'Sit up if you want a drink.'

It was a struggle for Moccasin Joe but he made it. His eyes were still a little hazy, but clear enough to look at Baylor with hatred.

Baylor took the knife from the fire and stood over his captive, tapping his boot against the man's bare foot. Moccasin Joe looked at the glowing steel, and then at Baylor. His eyes showed no fear.

'You ain't got the guts.'

The bluff was no good. Baylor drove the knife into the ground near the fire. 'I've got guts enough to help hang you,' he said. 'We know you're one of the rustlers, and we know you've been doing chores for the Thing in the basin that's killed our men. Better loosen up, Joe.'

'My name ain't Joe.'

'That won't make any difference when you swing.'

'Talk away, cowboy.'

He's not afraid of me, Baylor thought, but it's up in his neck because of what he knows is out there.

It's out there, the night said.

Paxton should be coming. He should have been here an hour ago.

He went to the edge of the park, listening for the hoof sounds of the dun. There was nothing in the park but ancient night and aching quiet. Grunting sounds and the cracking of twigs sent Baylor running back to the fire. Moccasin Joe was trying to get away, pushing himself by digging his heels into the ground. He had gone almost twenty feet.

Baylor hauled him back to the fire. The man's muscles were jerking. 'They'll kill me,' he said, 'but that'll be the best way. Put out the fire. I'll tell you!'

'You've pulled a couple of fast ones already.'

'Put it out!'

Brutal fear came like a bad odor from the man. Baylor's back was crawling. He turned toward the creek to get another hatful of water.

Twigs popped. Something thudded softly out in the forest.

'It's coming! Turn me loose!' Moccasin Joe's voice rose in a hoarse, quavering scream. 'O Jesus . . .' And then he was silent.

Standing at the edge of firelight, with his bent-barrelled pistol in his hand, Baylor was in a cold sweat.

Paxton's voice came from the forest. 'Baylor!'

'Here!' Baylor made two efforts before he got the pistol back in leather. By the time Paxton came in, leading the dun, Baylor's fear had turned to anger.

'Did you make another trip out to visit and have a shave!'

Paxton was in no light mood, either. His face was swelling from mosquito bites. He had clawed at them and smeared mud from his hairline to his throat. 'I got bogged down in a stinking swamp! Lost your carbine there, too.' He looked at Moccasin Joe. 'I see you got— What ails him?'

Moccasin Joe's eyes were set, unseeing. His jaw was jerking and little strings of saliva were spilling into his beard.

Mice feet tracked on Baylor's spine. 'Umm!' he said in a long breath. 'He thought you were the Thing!'

'The Thing! Good God!' Paxton's eyes rolled white in his mud-smeared face. His voice dropped. 'Your horse raised hell back there a minute ago.'

The dun was shuddering now, its ears set toward the creek. It was ready to bolt. Paxton drew his pistol.

'Put that popgun away!' Baylor cried. 'Help me get him on the horse!' He grabbed the knife and slashed the belt around Joe's ankles. 'Stand up!'

The man rose obediently, numbly, his jaw still working. Paxton leaped to grab the dun's reins when the horse tried to bolt toward the park.

Baylor threw Moccasin Joe across the saddle of the plunging horse.

'Lead the horse out of here!'

They crashed toward the park, with the horse fighting to get away, with Baylor fighting to keep Moccasin Joe across the saddle. The dun tried to bolt until they were in timber at the lower end of the park, and then it quieted.

'How far to the cabin where Raven is?' Baylor asked.

'Maybe four miles,' Paxton answered. 'I won't try no short cuts through a swamp this time.' He laughed shakily.

They spoke but little as they moved through the deep night of Big Ghost Basin. Baylor walked behind now. Paxton broke off a limb and used it as a feeler overhead when they were in timber. Each time he said, 'Limb!' they heard Moccasin Joe grunt a little as he ducked against the horn.

Baylor guessed it was well after midnight when Paxton stopped in the rocks and said, 'It's close to here—some place. I'll go ahead and see.'

Baylor was alone. He heard Paxton's footsteps fade into the rocks. The dun was droop-headed now. Moccasin Joe was a dark lump in the saddle.

Relief ran through Baylor when he heard the mumble of voices somewhere ahead, and presently Paxton came back. 'The cabin is about a hundred yards from here. Raven's there.'

Paxton took care of the dun. Raven and Baylor led the captive inside. Moccasin Joe was like a robot. Light from a brass Rivers lamp showed a four-bunk layout, with a large fireplace at one end. There was a shelf of books near the fireplace, and rock specimens scattered everywhere else.

Raven's hair was rumpled. He was in his undershirt and boots. His pink face was shining and his eyes were sharp. He looked at Moccasin Joe and said, 'I thought *I* brought in specimens.'

Moccasin Joe was staring.

Raven took the man's right hand and looked at the grated knuckles. He stood on tiptoe to peer at the marks where Baylor had banged Moccasin Joe's head against the rock.

'I roughed him up,' Baylor said.

'You didn't hurt him.' Raven passed his hand before the man's face. 'Oregon! Oregon!' he said.

'Huh?' the man said dully.

'You know him?' Baylor asked.

'I saw him out on the west prairie, camped with a group of men. They called him that.'

'Rustlers, huh?'

'Probably. I ride where I like. Nobody bothers me. I've doctored a man or two out that way, without asking his business.'

'What's wrong with this one?' Baylor asked.

'Shock. His mind, roughly, is locked on something. Did you try to scare him to death?'

'Not me. Something scared the hell out of me, and Paxton, too. Maybe if we'd known what it was, we'd be like Mocc—Oregon.'

Paxton came in. Raven glanced at his face. 'Wash it off, and quit scratching the lumps,

143

Paxton. Get some grease out of that jar there by the books.' Raven motioned Oregon toward a chair. 'Sit down there.'

Doc Raven went to work. He cleansed and dressed Oregon's hand, and took care of the cuts on his head, shearing into the long hair with evident satisfaction. 'Retire!' he muttered. 'I've got so I don't go to an outbuilding without taking a medical kit along.'

Raven was completely happy, Baylor thought.

'Help yourselves to the grub, boys,' the doctor said.

Oregon ate mechanically, staring at Raven most of the time. When Raven was briskly directing him into a bunk afterward, the doctor asked casually, 'Did Martin get over that dislocated shoulder all right?'

'Yeah,' Oregon said. 'Yeah, he's all right,' and then his eyes slipped back to dullness once more.

Raven looked at Paxton and Baylor. 'I think he'll be coming out of it after a night's rest. Go to bed. I'll just sit here and read.'

'I don't want that man to get away,' Baylor said. 'He's going to tell me something in the morning.'

Raven shook his head. 'You won't get anything out of this one, Baylor. I probed two bullets out of his chest once, and he never made a peep.'

Raven smiled at the suspicious stares of the two ranchers. 'I'm a doctor,' he said. 'Retired.' He laughed. 'Now go to bed, both of you.'

Raven was cooking when Baylor woke up. Paxton was still sound asleep. Oregon was lying in his bunk awake. There was complete awareness in his eyes when he looked at Baylor.

Baylor said, 'Ready to talk?'

'To hell with you,' Oregon said.

Paxton woke up while Baylor was dressing. He took his pistol from under his blankets and walked across the room to Oregon. 'That was my brother that was killed by your pet a few days ago.'

'Too bad,' Oregon said.

Paxton turned toward Baylor. 'Let's stake this bastard out by a fire tonight—and leave him!'

'That's enough!' Raven's voice cut sharply. 'Oregon is yours, but let's have no more of that kind of talk.'

'What'll we do?' Paxton asked. 'I want to go with you to meet Sherry this morning, and—' He glanced at Raven.

'You stay here,' Baylor said. 'I'll see Sherry. What the hell does she want?'

The first hot meal in several days was like water in a desert. After breakfast Baylor brought the dun from a barred enclosure where a spring made a green spot in the rocks.

Paxton grumped about being left to watch

145

the prisoner. Sherry would take some of that out of him soon enough, after they were married, Baylor thought.

Baylor went inside for one last word with Oregon. 'I know you lied about your bunch hanging out on the reservation, Oregon. How about Kreider?'

'You find out,' Oregon said.

Baylor looked at Paxton.

'Don't fret,' Paxton said. 'I'll watch him, all right.'

Raven walked outside with him. 'I know how you boys feel, Baylor. Out here you try to make things all black or all white. There's shades between the two, Baylor. I don't defend Oregon. I don't condemn him. You understand?'

'I'm trying to.'

'That helps. You want my rifle?'

'Carbine.' Baylor shook his head. 'Thanks, no.'

Sherry and Gary Owen were waiting in Battleground Park when he reached there. It was close to where Bill Paxton had been killed.

'What happened to your nose?' Sherry asked.

'Froze it in the creek. Nice place you picked to meet me.'

'Yeah.' Owen looked toward the little mound that covered the fire site. 'She picked it.'

Sherry said, 'Did you see anyone last night?'

'Pierce and me met a man, not socially, though. Who do you mean?'

'Any of the ranchers, tight-mouth. They came in last night, the crews from every outfit. Crosby and Baldray got them together. They're going to filter around and trap the rustlers tomorrow or the next day near the Wall.'

'Baldray's idea?' Baylor asked.

Owen nodded. 'Him and Kreider.'

'Kreider!'

'He's a special agent of the Indian Department,' Owen said. 'He was sent here to investigate a rumor that the rustlers were operating from reservation land. For a while he was in solid with them. From what we gathered, he's got a chum still with the bunch on the west prairie, and that fellow tipped Kreider off about the next raid.'

The rustlers must have caught on to Kreider, Baylor thought. That was why Oregon had been so willing to identify him as one of the gang. Tomorrow or the next day . . . Plenty of time for what Baylor had to do. He looked at a .45–90 Winchester in Owen's saddle boot.

'I'd like to borrow your rifle, Gary.'

'I brought one for you,' Sherry said. She walked into the grass and returned with a double-barreled weapon.

Baylor hefted the piece. 'One of Baldray's.'

'Elephant gun,' Sherry said. 'A .577, whatever that is.' She gave her brother, one by one, a half-dozen cartridges. 'Pierce told me he saw the track of something down here that scared him. Where is Pierce?'

His sister was quite a woman, Baylor thought. He told her and Owen about capturing Oregon. 'I figure it will be easier to get a line on this Thing, now that Oregon is out of the way.'

Owen stared at the timber edges of the park. 'Thing,' he muttered. 'I'll stay with you, Ken.'

'Take Sherry back to the benches—'

'I know the way,' Sherry said. 'You know something? Kreider says there's a bill going into the next Congress to make Big Ghost public land again.'

'Owen's taking you back to the benches,' Baylor said.

'You know who got action started on that bill?' Sherry asked. 'Jim Baldray.'

'Yeah,' Owen said. 'Even Kullhem admits now that he must have had the wrong idea about Baldray. I'll stay down here with you, Ken.'

'The two of you work well together,' Baylor said, 'changing the subject, throwing me off. All right, get out of here, Sherry, and be sure you're good and out before night.'

The girl got on her horse. Her face was pale under its tan. 'Don't depend entirely on that elephant gun, Ken. Get up in a tree, or something.'

'I figured on that,' Baylor said. 'So long, Red.'

The two men watched until she disappeared into the timber at the upper end of Battleground Park.

'Fighting rustlers don't scare me no more than a man's got a right to be scared,' Owen said abruptly. He dug out his short-stemmed pipe and lit it. 'But after I saw Paxton—and them other two, I'll admit I didn't have the guts to come down here at night. Now I'm here, I'll stay.'

Baylor was glad to have him—with that big-bored Winchester.

'I don't know what we're after,' Baylor said. 'But maybe in a couple of hours we'll know. Come on.'

They went back in the timber, and stayed out of sight until they came to the park below the burn, the place where Baylor had built his fire the night before. The memory of the night began to work on Baylor.

He felt a chill when he saw that the fire he and Paxton had left burning in their quick retreat had been covered with a great heap of dirt and needles. There were long marks in the torn ground, but no sharp imprints. The story was there. The fire had kept on smoldering under the first weight of dirt and dry forest mat, and the Thing had continued to throw dirt in a savage frenzy until the smoke had ceased. Fire. That was the magnet.

Owen sucked nervously on his pipe, staring. 'What done it?'

Baylor shook his head. 'Let's try the soft ground by the creek.' They stood on the east bank. Baylor stared at the choke of willows and trees on the other side. Last night he had dipped water from this very spot, and over there somewhere the Thing had been pacing, circling, working up to coming in. It must have been quite close when he threw Oregon at the dun and ran in terror.

Night will come again, the voices said.

Baylor and Owen stayed close together while they searched. Farther up the stream they found where the Thing had leaped the creek in one bound. Four imprints in the muddy bank.

'I'll be dipped in what!' There was a little fracture in Owen's voice. 'That ain't no track of nothing I ever seen!'

The outlines were mushy. The mud was firm, but still there was no clear definition of form. The whole thing was a patchwork of bumps and ridges that would not fit any living creature Baylor had even seen or heard of. 'That's no bear,' he said.

'Back in Ireland my grandmother used to scare us . . .' Owen shook his head.

On a limb snag across the creek they found a small patch of short, brittle hair with a scab scale clinging to it.

'There ain't nothing in the world with hair

like that!' Owen cried.

Here with the shroud moss motionless on gray limbs, in the ancient stillness of Big Ghost, Baylor was again prey to fear of the Unknown, and for a moment there was no civilization because nothing fitted previous experience.

'The rustlers have seen it,' he said. 'Oregon said it got one of their men. They wouldn't have covered up for it if they hadn't been afraid we might recognize the sign.' He stared at Owen. 'Fire, Gary. Fire is what brings it!'

'I been here at night—with fire.' Owen hunched his shoulders.

'It's a big hole. A man might be lucky here for a long time, and then one night . . . Where are the ranchers going to meet?'

'They'll camp out in little bunches on those timbered hogbacks that point toward the West Wall. When they see Crosby's smoke signal from the Wall—'

'We've got to warn them, Gary. Orahood never spent a night out in his life without building a fire. Get down there and pass the word—no fires!'

'That leaves you alone.'

'I've been several nights alone. Take the dun with you. I don't want him hurt.'

'Holy God, Ken! You don't want the dun hurt, but you—'

'Stick to the timber, Gary, so you won't mess up their trap.'

Baylor took both ropes from the saddles. Ready to leave, Owen said, 'Take my rifle. That elephant business only shoots twice.'

'I'll do better than that, from where I'll be. Tonight you'll like the feel of that big barrel across your knees, Gary.'

'Don't scare me. I already know I'm a damned coward. I *want* to leave here. I'll admit it.' Owen rode away.

Baylor did not like to admit how alone he felt.

Big Ghost nights always seemed to settle as if they had a special purpose in making the basin a black hole. From his platform of laced rope between two limbs of a spruce tree, Baylor peered down to where his pile of wood was ready for a match. He had pulled in other fuel close to the site, enough to keep a fairly large fire all night.

It was about time to light it. The sooner the better. The smoke would make a long trail through the forest, the flames a little bright spot in the murk, and this Thing that must kill fire might be attracted. It would be a cinch from here.

A cinch? Maybe the Thing climbs trees.

Baylor climbed down and lit the fire. He waited just long enough to know that it would burn, and then he climbed again to his rope perch.

The blackness laughed at his haste.

Smoke came up between the ropes and

began to choke him. That was a point he had not thought of at all; but presently the fire took hold in earnest, light reached out to touch the gray holes of waiting trees, and a small wind began to drift the smoke at a lower level.

Baylor tried to settle comfortably against the ropes. The sling of the heavy double-barrel was over a limb above him, so the weapon could not fall. The four spare cartridges were buttoned in the breast pocket of his jumper. He felt the cold, big roundness of them when he took out the makings of a cigarette.

It was as dark as a pocket up in the tree. For a while the oddness of being where he was intrigued Baylor, and then he thought of a dozen flaws in his plan. But if it did not work tonight, he would stay with it until it did. He reached over to touch the .577. The four spare cartridges did not count. He had two shots coming. They should be enough.

Bill Paxton's forty-five was empty when Kreider found him.

The night lagged. Big Ghost gathered all its secrets to it, and the darkness whispered. Three times Baylor went down to put wood on the fire. Each time he took the heavy rifle, and each time his flesh crawled until he was back on the rope net once more.

He smoked all his tobacco. Thirst started. He listened to the creek. It was not very far.

Go get yourself a drink, Baylor.

He tried not to listen. His thirst grew out of all proportions, and he knew it was not real. He could not be thirsty; he had drunk just before dark.

Get yourself a drink. Don't be a fool.

He waited till the fire needed wood. After building it up, he stood a moment by the tree, with one hand on the rope that led to safety.

Go on, Baylor. Are you afraid to get a drink?

The water was icy cold against the sweat on his face. He drank from cupped hands, then wiped them on his jumper, staring at the blackness across the creek. Last night the Thing had been somewhere out there. It might be there now.

He took two steps toward the fire. Something splashed in the water behind him. He was cocking the gun and swinging around all the time he knew the splash had come from a muskrat.

For a few moments he stood drying his hands over the heat, a little gesture of striking back at the Unknown. But when he started up the tree he went all the way with a rush.

In the cold hours long after midnight he was on the ground tending the fire when he heard a soft sound beyond the limits of the light. He unslung the rifle and felt the thumping of his heart.

It's there. It's watching you.

He turned toward the tree. He heard the crush of dry pine needles. He cocked the gun

154

and backed toward the tree, feeling behind him for the rope. Something moved on the edge of firelight. An enormous, shadowy form emerged from blackness. It rocked from side to side. A hoarse roar enveloped Baylor.

He fired the right barrel, and then the left. The Thing came in, bellowing. Straight across the fire it charged, scattering embers. Baylor had another cartridge out, but he dropped it and clubbed the rifle. He was completely stripped now of all the thinking of evolved and civilized man.

The bellowing became a strangled grunt. The Thing was down, its hind legs in the flames. It tried to crawl toward Baylor, and then it was still. Baylor rammed another cartridge in and fired a third shot. The great bulk took the fearful impact without stirring.

Cordite rankness was in Baylor's nostrils as he kicked embers back toward the fire and put on fuel with shaking hands. The stench of burning hair sickened him. He pulled the flames away from the hind legs of the beast.

He had known what he was up against from the moment the animal had stood higher than a horse there on the edge of firelight, then dropped to the ground to charge. He had killed a grizzly bear.

When the flames were high he examined it. The feet were huge, misshapen, lacking the divisions of pads. All four were tortured, scrambled flesh that had fused grotesquely after being cruelly burned. Along the back and on one side of the bear were scabby patches where the hair had come back crisp and short. Around the mouth the flesh was lumpy, hideous from scar tissue. The jaws had been seared so terribly that the fangs and front teeth had dropped out.

He lifted one of the forelegs with both hands. There were traces of claws, some ingrown, the others brittle, undeveloped fragments.

The forest fire several years before! The bear had been a cub then, or perhaps half grown. The poor devil, caught by the flames, probably against the rocks, since only one side was scarred. He pictured it whimpering as it covered its face with its forepaws. And then, when it could no longer stand the pain and fear, it must have gone loping wildly across the burning forest mat.

Before it recovered it must have been a skinny, tortured brute. No wonder it had gone crazy afterward at the smell and sight of flames.

He found one of his bullet holes in the throat. That had to be the first shot, when the grizzly had been erect. The other must be in the shoulder that was underneath, and it would take a horse and rope to make sure. He cut into a lump on the shoulder that was up. Just a few inches below the tough hide, under the fat, he found a .45 bullet. One of Bill

Paxton's, probably.

That was enough examination. The poor, damned thing.

He was asleep by a dead fire when the savage crackling of gunfire roused him shortly after dawn. He sat up quickly. The firing ran furiously, somewhere near the Wall. Then the sounds dwindled to single cracks, at intervals. A little later Big Ghost was quiet.

Baylor hoped there was truth in what Owen had said about the basin going back to range. For the first time in days he heard the wakening sounds of birds. Before, he had been listening for something else.

He was asleep in the sun out in the park when the clatter roused him. The ranchers were coming out. Kullhem, his left arm in a sling, was riding with Baldray in the lead. Farther back, a man was tarpaulin-draped across his saddle.

Owen and Paxton spurred ahead to Baylor, who pointed toward the tarpaulin.

'Orahood,' Owen said. 'The only man we lost.'

Baylor was stabbed by the thought of Orahood's wife alone at Sky Hook, with a baby coming on.

Paxton said, 'We caught 'em foul on Windy Trail! We broke their backs!'

'Oregon?' Baylor asked.

'He tried one of his little tricks.'

Owen kept looking toward the forest.

'It's there,' Baylor said wearily.

Men gathered around the grizzly.

'Good Lord!' Crosby kept saying. 'Would you look at the size of that!'

'That must have been a spot of fun, eh, Baylor?' Baldray frowned, not satisfied with his words. 'You know I mean a narrow place— a tight one.'

Raven was all around the bear, like a fly. 'Unusually fine condition,' he mused. 'How did he get food while he was recovering from those burns?'

'He healed himself in a swamp,' Kullhem growled. 'There's always cows and calves bogged down in the swamps.'

'A remarkable specimen, nonetheless.' Raven drew a sheath knife. 'I'll have a look at that stomach and a few other organs.' He hesitated. 'Your bear, of course, Baylor. You don't mind?'

'Yeah.' Baylor shook his head slowly. 'Leave him be, Raven. The poor devil suffered enough when he was alive.'

Raven stood up reluctantly. He put his knife away. 'I guess I understand.'

Baldray's bony face showed that he understood. 'Fire killer,' he said. 'The poor damned beast.'

THE SINGING SANDS

There were three passes ahead and their names were like the rhythm of a chant, Mosca, Medano and Music. The alliteration kept running in Johnny Anderson's mind as his tired pony chopped through the rabbitbrush, across alkali flats where the dust rose thin and bitter in the windless air. Like magic words that would kill the trouble behind, the names chased each other; but every few moments Anderson looked across his shoulder at the long backtrail.

Jasper Lamb was doing the same thing, twisting wearily in the saddle, squinting his bloodshot eyes at the gray distance. He was a middle-aged man, slouching, leanly built. For a year Anderson had prowled the mountains with him. They had never faced any severe test until now; and now Anderson was wondering if he had picked the right partner. Lamb was not showing the proper concern about things.

Anderson worked his lips and ran his tongue around his mouth to clear dust and the cottony feeling that had been in his mouth ever since he knew there were men on their trail. 'Which pass, Lamb?'

'Medano, I know it best.' Lamb glanced at the heavily loaded mule he was towing. The mule was the strongest of the three animals,

159

but it would not be hurried.

Each mile seemed to bring them no closer to the mountains with their golden streaks of frost-touched aspens. Looking backward at the space they had crossed, Anderson was uneasy because of the very emptiness. He said hopefully, 'Maybe we threw them off when we made that fake toward Poncha Pass early this morning.'

'I figured on wind,' Lamb said. 'There ain't been any. We've left a trail like a single furrow ploughed across a field. The wind blows like old Scratch here sometimes, but today it didn't.' He had come out during the Pike's Peak bust, cutting his teeth on the mountains and losing his illusions at the same time, so now he did not rail against luck or the weather. 'They'll be along.'

Johnny Anderson was young. He had passed his twenty-second birthday the week before when they were making their final clean-up on their placer claim in the San Juan. He wasted energy cursing the vagaries of the weather; but half his anger was fear as he saw how Lamb's buckskin was limping. The horse had thrown a shoe in the rocky foothills just north of the Rio Grande the night before. Anderson tried to weigh the limp against the distance yet to go; and then he turned to look behind.

There was no dust far back. Mosca, Medano and Music... He studied immense buff foothills ahead. He had never seen their like before but he was not greatly interested.

He asked, 'Who are they, do you suppose?'

Lamb did not waste motion in shrugging or any other gesture. 'You saw some of the toughs there in Baker's Park when we stopped overnight. Pick any bunch of them.'

'We made a mistake!' Anderson said. 'We shouldn't have stopped there, and then we guarded the panniers on the mule too close. We should have dumped them on the ground like they didn't amount to nothing. We made another mistake when we slipped out of there by night. We—'

'Sure, we made mistakes.' Lamb leaned ahead to feel the shoulder of his horse. 'We come out of the San Juan with a loaded mule at the end of summer. Nobody had to be smart to know what we're carrying.' He kept watching the buckskin's shoulder. 'We made our pile in a hurry, boy. I mistrust too much good luck.'

Anderson let the thought grind away for a while. 'Is your horse going to make it?'

'I doubt it, not without he rests and I try to do something for that tender foot.' Lamb looked at the unshod Indian pony under Anderson. It cut no figure at all beside the buckskin. It rode hard and its gait was uneven but the mustang mark was there and there were guts in the pony for many miles yet. Lamb watched it for a moment with no expression on his bearded, dusty features.

Slowly the great pale brown hills came closer. No trees, no rocks broke the rounding contours. The ridges were sharp on the spines, delicately molded. The shadings of the coloration flowed so subtly into each other that Anderson could not tell whether the hills were a quarter of a mile away or two miles. The whole mass of them seemed to pulse in the still heat. Anderson's sudden loss of distance judgment gave him a queer feeling.

When he looked behind once more and saw only lonely vastness, the claws of fear began to loosen and the hills began to capture his attention. A gentle incline led the two men among the pinon trees. The pitchy scent of them was warmly strong. Lamb swung his sore-footed horse into a broad gulch and soon they were riding on a brown carpet that flowed out from the skirts of the hills. Pure sand.

The pack mule balked the moment its hooves touched the silky softness. It sniffed and held back on the tow rope, but at last Lamb urged it on ahead. Riding in an eerie silence broken only by the gentle plopping of hooves, the two men struck a course to turn the shoulder of the dunes where they ended against the mountains.

'That's the biggest pile of sand I ever saw!' Anderson said.

In the strike of the afternoon sun the sweeping curves of the hills blended into a oneness that robbed Anderson of depth perception. There were moments when the dunes had only height and length. He estimated the highest ridge at seven hundred feet, but it seemed so far away he guessed that a man could not reach it in a day.

Staring at the dunes, he forgot for a time the threat behind him—until Lamb stopped the buckskin suddenly. The dust was out there now, standing like thin smoke above the rabbitbrush on the way that they had come. As they watched, the first wind of the day came out of the southwest. The claws hooked in again and the tightness returned to Anderson's stomach.

He rode to the rear of the pack mule, thinking to urge it into greater speed when they started. Lamb's calmness stopped him. With one eye almost closed so that the side of his mouth was raised in the semblance of a smile, Lamb was slouching in the saddle and studying the dust as if not sure of the cause of it. He scrubbed the scum from his teeth with his tongue.

'There were five of them before,' he said. 'Guess there's still that many. You know something, Andy? They swung away this morning to get fresh horses at Pascual's ranch.' Lamb eyed Anderson's wiry scrub. He glanced to the right, past cotton woods and pinon trees, up to where Mosca Pass trail came down in a V of the mountains. 'Medano is still best for us. Once we hit the Huerfano, I've got more friends among the Mexicans than a cur has fleas.'

'Let's go!'

Lamb swung down. 'My horse won't last two miles.'

'He's got to! We'll get to the rocks and stand 'em off.'

'We might do that with Indians, yes.' Lamb lifted the buckskin's left forefoot and looked at the hoof. 'These are white men, Andy.' He let the hoof drop. 'They know what we got.' He walked to a cottonwood at the edge of the gulch.

'White men or not, by God—'

'I ain't aiming to die over no gold,' Lamb said. 'I've got along too many years without it. I ain't figuring to let them have it either.' He grinned and his toughness was never more apparent. 'Just wait a spell. The wind is coming.'

'Out in the valley it would have helped, but here, when we hit the trees—'

'Wait,' Lamb said.

The wind reached them after a while. Strong and warm it came out of the southwest. There was an odd rustling sound and the sand lay out in streamers from the ridges of the dunes. It was difficult to tell about the dust cloud, but Anderson knew it must be closer.

All at once Anderson realized that the tracks he and Lamb had made in the broad

164

gulch were gone. Unbroken sand that lay in gentle waves like frozen brown water covered every mark they had made since entering the gulch.

Lamb led his buckskin and the mule toward the dunes. The idea ran then in Anderson's mind that they would lose their pursuers by circling through the hollows of the hills; but when the animals struck the first ridge and began to labor in the shifting, slippery sand, he knew his thought was wrong.

They ploughed over the ridge and dropped into a small basin where the ground was bare. All around the edges of the hollow the sand was skirling, running in tiny riffles, and up on the great hills above them it was whipping from the spines in two different directions.

Lamb took the mule close to the side of the bowl where the sand came down steeply. He began to take the gold from the panniers. It was in wheels, circular pieces of buckskin gathered from the outside edge and tied with thongs. When the first few sacks dropped at the edge of the sand Anderson cried a protest.

'I'd rather fight for it!'

'I'd rather live,' Lamb said. 'We're not going to get clear unless I ride the mule. We'll get a little fighting even then. Give me a hand.'

Each sack that thudded down was a wrench at Anderson's heart. He could not remember how easily the gold had come to them from a rich pocket in the San Juan; he could only estimate the weight of each sack as it fell at the edge of the fine silt.

'Not all of it, for God's sake!' he cried.

Lamb kept dropping the buckskin sacks. 'Take what you want but remember you're riding a tired horse. Even Indian nags play out, Andy.' A few moments later when Lamb saw his partner stuffing sacks under his shirt, he said, 'It'll be here when we come back, son.'

It was not the words, but sudden wild music, that brought Anderson's head up with a jerk. It was a weird and whining sound, the bow of the wind playing across the sand strings of the ridges high above. Anderson listened only long enough to recognize what the sound was. It was mocking, discordant. He stuffed more gold inside his shirt.

When the panniers that had held almost two hundred pounds of weight were flapping loosely against the mule, Lamb's voice snapped across the wind with the crack of urgency, 'Rake the sand down on top of the stuff while I shift my saddle to the mule.'

Soft and warm, the sand slid easily under Anderson's raking hands. When he had covered part of the long row of sacks the wind had already concealed the marks where he had clawed. They climbed from the hollow, pausing on the ridge to peer through a brown haze at the dust still coming toward them. Anderson turned then to look into the little basin. All marks were gone, but he did not trust the smooth quickness of the sand.

'Maybe we could stand them off here,' he said.

'Maybe we could die of thirst here, too.' Lamb pointed across the shallow sand to the edge of the gulch. 'It was six hundred and ten long steps, Andy, from that cottonwood with the busted top. Sight above the tree to that patch of gray rocks on the mountains. You got it?'

Anderson tried to burn the marks into his mind. He stared until he found a third point of sighting, the smoke-gray deadness of a spruce tree between the cottonwood and the patch of rocks. Six hundred and ten paces from the cottonwood. He could never forget this place.

Out in the rabbitbrush the riders had dropped into a swale. Only the dust they had raised behind them was visible. Lamb swung up on the mule and the mule tried to pitch him off. 'I hope we never have to eat this devil,' he said, 'as tough as he is.' He rode down the slope and into the broad expanse of shallow sand, towing his limping buckskin.

Anderson had difficulty in mounting. His shirt bulged with weight and his boots were full of sand. The hills were singing their high, queer song. He rode away, twisted in the saddle to watch his tracks; and he saw them drifting into smoothness almost as quickly as he made them. The treasure was safe enough but he worried because there seemed to be a gloating tone in the singing sands.

Now the dust was much closer and the fear of men was greater than all other worries.

Beside the eastern shoulder of the hills they crossed ground where water had carried brown earth from the mountains. The earth was cracked and curled upward in little chips. They let the animals drink when they hit the first seep of Medano Creek.

'Now we got our work cut out,' Lamb said.

Medano Pass was rocky. The wind was funneling through it cold and sharp. Now the pursuers gained in earnest, for Anderson's pony began to lag and the hobbling buckskin began to lay back stubbornly on the lead rope.

From a high switchback Anderson saw the riders for the first time. Five of them, the same as before. 'Let's get rid of the damned buckskin, Lamb!'

'About another mile and then we will.'

When they came to a place where the trail was very narrow above a booming creek, Lamb said, 'Drop a sack of gold here, Andy. The lead man will have to get down to get it. Every minute will help.'

'Drop one of your own.'

'I got only one,' Lamb said patiently.

The gold was a terrible weight around Anderson's middle but he would not drop a sack. Nor would he part with it when he had to dismount to lead his pony up steep pitches. The sides of the horses were pounding. They stopped to rest at the top of a brutal hill. They could hear the sounds of the men behind them. Anderson tried to pull off his boots but the sand had worked so tightly around his feet and ankles that he could not get the boots off, and he was afraid to spend too much time in trying.

On a ledge above a canyon Lamb stopped again. He took the panniers from the buckskin, dropped a heavy rock into each of them, and hurled them away. He stripped the packsaddle and threw it by the cinch strap. Anderson heard it crash somewhere in the rocks out of sight. In the next stand of aspens Lamb took the buckskin out of sight and turned it loose.

He seemed to be gone a long time. Anderson stood beside his trembling pony with his rifle ready, watching the trail. Lamb returned. His face was grim with the first anger he had shown since the pursuit began. He took his rifle and walked down the trail. 'Go on,' he ordered. 'I'll be along directly.'

Anderson went ahead on foot. There were seven shots, flat reports that sent echoes through the rocks. Anderson stopped, waiting, afraid. Presently Lamb came trotting up the trail. Blood was dripping from his left hand and his shirt was ripped above the elbow. He whipped the blood off his hand and said, 'Get on, don't wait for nothing. Not far ahead they got a chance to flank around us if we stop to pick flowers.'

On the next steep, narrow pitch Anderson dropped a sack of gold. It was a place where horses would have to hold in a straining position against the grade while the lead man got down. It was not much, but maybe it would help. Four more times he picked his spots and dropped more sacks.

Twice more Anderson went back on foot with his rifle. There were fewer shots each time.

Sunset dripped its colors on the mountains and they flamed with the hue that gave them their name, *Sangre de Cristo*, Blood of Christ. The colors died and the cold dusk came. Again Lamb went back on the trail and his rifle made crimson flashes. They passed the place where a Spanish governor had camped an avenging army two centuries before. They went over the top and the necks of the animals slanted downward.

It was dark then. A wind that came from vastness was running up the mountain. To Anderson, the pass had been the obstacle, and now they were across it. He breathed relief. The magic words, Mosca, Medano and Music came again; but moments later he forgot that it was his life he had worried about, and he thought of the gold they had left in the sand, and of the sacks of gold they had dropped on the trail. At least he had not thrown away everything; there were two sacks yet inside his shirt.

A pale moon rose, throwing ghostly light on the rocks. Far below the timber was a black sea. It was still a long way to the Huerfano, and there were things like weariness and hunger.

Lamb said, 'Hold up a second.'

In the dead stillness they heard the sound of hoofs sliding on stones on the trail behind them. The men were still coming. Not knowing who they were made it worse for Anderson. Their persistence chilled him. Lamb was a dark form near the head of the mule. 'One of those three knows this trail,' he muttered.

There had been five men. Anderson did not comment on the difference.

Lamb listened a moment longer. 'They're on a short-cut that I didn't care to try.' For the first time he sounded worried. He mounted and sent the mule down the trail on the trot.

The clatter of stones came loudly on the higher benches of the mountain.

Lamb set a dangerous pace, cutting across the sharp angles of the switchbacks, sending rocks in wild flight down the slopes. They made a long turn to the left and entered timber on the edge of a canyon where a waterfall was splashing in the moonlight. At the head of the canyon the trail swung back to the right. They were then in dense timber where the needle mat took sharpness from the hoofbeats of the horses.

'Hold it,' Lamb called back softly, and then he stopped.

Above the canyon they had skirted, where the trail lay in Z patterns against the mountain, Anderson heard the riders. Suddenly there was an eerie quietness.

Lamb said, 'Just ahead of us the trail is open to the next point. They can reach us good from where they are.' He led the mule aside. 'Put your horse across first but don't follow him too close.'

Anderson pulled his rifle free. From the edge of the timber the trail ahead lay against cliffs of white quartz. It seemed starkly exposed and lighted. He peered up the mountain. The shadows were tricky among the huge rocks and he could make out nothing. But then he heard a tired horse blow from somewhere up there in the rocks.

He prodded his pony into the open. It went a few slow paces and stopped. With savage force he bounced a rock off its rump. The animal jumped and started on at a half trot.

Anderson ran. He heard the crashing of the rifles and from the corner of his eye he saw their flame. They seemed to be a long way off but yet he heard the smack of lead against the cliffs beside him. The pony was almost to the point when its hind legs went down. It screamed in agony and pawed its way along the ledge. It reared halfway up, twisting. Anderson saw the glint of moonlight on steel

172

where the leather was worn off the horn, and that was when the pony was going into the canyon.

A man on the mountainside yelled triumphantly, 'We got the mule!'

Then Anderson was across. He fell behind the rocky point and shot toward the sound of the voice. The horses were moving up there in the rocks now and someone was cursing. Anderson rammed in another cartridge and fired.

The mule came with a rush, nearly trampling him before he could roll aside and leap up. He caught the bridle with a desperate lunge when the animal would have jogged on down the trail. Soon afterward Lamb skidded around the point. He knelt and fired. 'No good,' he muttered. 'Two of them got into the timber on foot.' He reloaded and stood up. 'Now let *them* try that trail.'

If there had been a taunt or a challenge from the black trees, Anderson would have been sure he was fighting men instead of some determined deadliness that would follow him forever. But the trees were silent.

'Take the mule,' Lamb said. 'He'll stay with the trail. By daylight you'll be seeing sheep. Ask the first herder you come to how to get to Luis Mendoza's place. Wait for me there.'

'We'll both—'

'I was ramming around these mountains when you was still wearing didies,' Lamb said.

173

'Listen to what I say, boy. Get to hell out of here with that mule. That's what they're after. They think the gold is still on it. We *want* 'em to think so because one of these days we've got to go back after it. Go on now.'

Anderson gave the mule its head and let it pick its way down the trail. He was a half hour away from the point when he heard the first shots rolling sullenly high above him. In the bleak, cold hours just before sun-up, he heard more shooting. And then the mountain was silent.

The two sheepherders sitting on a rock beside their flock in a high meadow eyed the mule keenly. 'Luis Mendoza?' They looked at each other. One of them pointed toward the valley. It went like that all morning, whenever Anderson stopped at adobes on the Huerfano. The liquid eyes sized up the mule and him, and weighed a consideration; but when he asked the way to Luis Mendoza's place, there was another careful weighing and he was pointed on.

The hot sun pressed him lower in the saddle. Sweat streaked down through the dust on his face, burning his eyes. At noon on this bright late-fall day he came into the yard of an adobe somewhat larger than the others he had passed. Hens were taking dust baths in the shade. There was a green field near the river, and goats upon a hill.

From the gloom of the house a deep voice

asked, 'Who comes?'

In Spanish Anderson said, 'I am the friend of Jasper Lamb.'

A little man walked from the house. His hair and mustache were white. His legs were short and bowed. From a nest of wrinkles around his eyes his gaze was like sharp, black points. He said, 'You are followed?'

'We were followed.'

'And Lamb?'

'He is in the mountains yet. He will come.' Anderson wondered if he ever would.

The little man said sharply, 'I am Luis Mendoza. Lamb is like my son. Do not doubt that he will be here. And now, you are welcome.'

Thereupon a half dozen Mexican men of various ages appeared. One of them said, 'Yes, it is the mule of Jasper Lamb.'

'I have eyes.' Mendoza's Spanish flowed rapidly then as he gave orders. Four men rode away, going slowly, chattering, obliterating the marks of Anderson's coming. He knew that if any of the three pursuers got past Jasper Lamb and reached the Huerfano, there would be only shrugs and muteness, or lies, to answer their questions.

'Go back for Lamb,' Anderson said.

'He will be well, that one,' Mendoza answered.

'He's wounded.'

'That has happened before, also. Now we

will take off your boots.'

One of the pursuers did come in late afternoon. Lying on a pile of blankets on a cool dirt floor, Anderson heard the man ride up. 'I look for a stolen mule, Mendoza.'

Anderson tried to judge the enemy by the voice. A young man, he thought; and he knew already that he was a dangerous, determined man.

'Of that I know nothing.'

Anderson clutched his rifle and started to get up. A broad Mexican sitting across the room from him shook his head and made cautioning gestures with his hands, and all the time he was grinning. After a moment Anderson recognized the wisdom of silence. For one thing, his feet were so scraped and sore and swollen from the sand that had been in his boots that he doubted if he could get across the room.

The man outside said, 'The mule came this way. It had a heavy load. The man was young, with sandy hair.'

'A *gringo* perhaps,' Mendoza said lazily. 'They do not stop for long on the Huerfano. The climate sometimes makes them ill,' his voice slurred on gently. 'Very ill.'

'He could be in your house.'

'I do not think so. My sons do not think so. My nephews do not think so.'

There was a long silence.

'This stealer of mules is gone toward the

Arkansas long ago, I think, although I did not see him,' Mendoza said. 'It is a long ride, my friend, and you are late now.'

'Many things are possible,' the pursuer answered, fully as easily as Mendoza had spoken. There was no defeat in his tone, but a cold patience that made Anderson wish he could get him in the sights of a rifle for an instant. 'It could be that he is gone toward the Arkansas, and it could be that he is in your house, in spite of what all your sons and nephews think. Since the vote is in your favor, Mendoza, I will go toward the Arkansas myself.'

'May God go with you,' Mendoza said politely.

The man rode away. After a time Anderson dozed and then he woke, clutching where the weight should have been inside his shirt.

'At the head of your bed, *senor*,' the man across the room murmured.

Anderson found the sacks and dragged them against him, and then he slept until sometime in the dead of night when he heard a terrible shout, soon followed by laughter.

Lamb had arrived. He was shouting for wine.

*   *   *

Anderson and Lamb stayed three weeks on the Huerfano. Lamb had married Mendoza's

177

oldest daughter ten years before. She had died in childbirth a year later. These were facts that Anderson had never known before.

It was a simple, easy life here in the hills. There were sheep in the upland country, with old men and young boys to watch them. Maize and squash grew in the fields. Anderson did not know where the wine came from but it was here, and every night there was dancing at Mendoza's place.

Quite easily Lamb fell into the routineless drift of the life. He slept when it was hot. He hunted when he was in the mood, ate when he was hungry, and during the long, cool evenings he danced with the best of them on the packed ground in front of Mendoza's house. He was no longer the cool, efficient man who had directed the running fight across Medano. He acted as if he had forgotten the gold lying at the foot of the great dunes.

'We can get it any time,' he told Anderson. 'What's the rush?' It seemed to Anderson that he was casting around for an excuse. 'It's best not to go back there anyway until that last fellow gives up. Only a week ago one of Luis' cousins saw him heading back over the pass.'

'Why didn't Luis' cousin shoot him?'

'Why should he? Why should anyone on the Huerfano ask for unnecessary trouble? They can scrape up family battles enough to keep 'em busy all their lives, if they want to.' Lamb went away to take a nap.

The change in him puzzled Anderson. Or was it a change? Lamb would have a man believe that he didn't care about that gold. Suspicion narrowed Anderson's mind. He fretted over the delay. He brooded about Lamb's motives; and he worried about the cold-voiced man who had followed the mule even after his companions were dead.

One day he could bear impatience no longer. He told Lamb he was going alone to the dunes.

'Hold your horses. The big *baile* comes off day after tomorrow. We'll leave then.' Lamb sighed.

They gave two sacks of gold to Luis Mendoza. It was too much, Anderson thought, but when Lamb parted with his sack carelessly, Anderson felt that he must match it. They rode away on good horses, towing the mule as before. Anderson was in his own saddle, brought down from the mountain by one of Mendoza's sons two days after the Indian pony had gone over the cliff. There were new elk hide panniers on the mule, and they surely must be advertising the purpose of the trip to every Mexican on the Huerfano, so Anderson thought.

'We'll go up the Arkansas and over Hayden Pass and then swing down to the sand hills,' Lamb said. 'It's possible that fellow caught on to the fact the mule was traveling light. He may have somebody waiting on Medano.'

179

Anderson said, 'I don't favor this running in circles.'

'I don't favor trouble, particularly not over a bunch of damned metal that grows wild in the mountains.'

'That's what brought you out here in the first place.'

'Yeah. Well, it was different then,' Lamb said. He was unusually silent, almost surly, during the first two days on the trail.

They watered the animals on San Luis Creek when they came down to the floor of the inland plateau. Thirty miles away the dunes were a pale brown mass. Once again they seemed to be no closer after hours of dusty traveling. As if in a stupor, Lamb stared at the sunset on the *Sangre de Cristo*.

Anderson wanted to travel as far into the night as it took to reach the dunes but Lamb overrode him. They camped. Anderson did not sleep well. He kept his rifle close and was sensitive to all of Lamb's small movements and sounds. During the night Lamb rose to go out to the animals when the mule fouled up his picket rope. He came back to the camp slowly, a lean, tall figure slouching through the night.

Anderson held back the trigger of his rifle and cocked the piece silently. Afterward, when Lamb walked past and settled into his blankets with a grunt, Anderson let the hammer down again, and lay with the tightness ebbing slowly out of him.

It seemed to Anderson that they lagged when they started down the valley the next day. At last he cried, 'You're in no hurry, damn it!'

'I ain't for a fact.' Lamb gave him an oblique glance. 'There's kinds of grief that I don't care to hurry into.'

'That last man, don't worry about him.'

'I ain't,' Lamb said. 'I'm worrying some about the other four.'

They approached the northern end of the dunes. After they encountered the first shallow drifting of sand out from the skirts, they rode for almost ten miles beside the hills before they reached the broad gulch at the mouth of Medano Creek.

Anderson felt a constriction of breath. He wanted to gallop ahead. Nothing was changed. He saw the narrow-leaf cottonwood with the broken top and from a wide angle the gray rocks on the mountain. Mosca, Medano and Music . . . He wanted to shout.

They left the horses at the cottonwood. Lamb was silent, almost sullen, as if there were no pleasure in this. He stayed at the cottonwood while Anderson led the mule out to the ridge and then part way up the side. When Anderson stopped to look back, he was pleased to see that his trail lay straight behind him and that he was almost in direct line with the sighting marks. He had to shift only a few feet until he had them lined up, the snag-topped cottonwood, the dead spruce and the gray rocks.

He called then to Lamb to start his pacing. Anderson counted the steps as his partner came toward him. Three hundred and fifty across the shallow sand, another hundred to where Anderson waited. The two men went together up the ridge. It seemed higher than before. The total was six hundred steps when Anderson whirled around to take another sighting. They were dead in line.

'Six hundred and ten?' he asked, and his voice cracked on the edge of panic.

'That's right,' Lamb answered, and a man could read anything into his tone.

Anderson kept plunging on, but he knew already, and it made him savage. There was no ridge. He was climbing a slope that led on and on toward the deceptive hollows and troughs of the soft, pale sand. The basin was gone. He was a hundred feet above the gold on sand that ran like water.

He sighted again and then he turned and ran up the dune until his lungs ached and his leg muscles became knots of fire. He fell, staring along the surface of the wind-etched slope. Far off to his left there was a hollow, swooping all the way down to natural ground, but the basin with the gold was deeply covered. There was trickery in this; he had known it when the hills sang their song to him.

Anderson got up and staggered back to

where Lamb was standing by the mule. 'It wasn't six hundred and ten steps, was it?'

Lamb shifted his rifle. 'Just what I said, Andy.'

'Tell me the truth!' Anderson cocked his rifle and swung the piece on Lamb.

'Our gold is covered up,' Lamb said. His squint was at once understanding and dangerous. 'We're standing smack on top of it. Lower that barrel. It's full of sand.'

Anderson let the barrel of his rifle tip down. Sand poured out in a silent stream. He let the tension off the hammer. 'You knew the wind would cover it up, Lamb!'

'No, I didn't. I never realized how much this sand moves.'

'We'll dig it out!' Anderson cried. 'I don't care how deep it is!'

Lamb sat down. 'We'll play hell trying to dig it out.' He scooped his hand into the dune. Not far under the surface the sand was dark from dampness. He watched the fine dry grains from the top slide back into the hole. 'It took a million years for the wind to make these hills. I guess the wind has got a right to do with them as it pleases. We'll never be able to dig ten feet down.'

'Oh yes we will! Underneath it's damp. It'll hold. We'll start at the toe of the hill and tunnel. We'll line the tunnel with boards. We'll—'

Lamb shook his head. 'Let me show you

183

something.' He dug with his hands, gouging long furrows downslope. The dark sand under the surface was damp for a short time only before the air dried it, and then it sloughed away. 'Your boards wouldn't help much, if we knew where to get them. They'd dry out brittle. They'd crack and the sand would pour through the cracks and knot-holes. If we were lucky enough to make twenty feet, one day the whole works would cave in on us.'

'You act like you don't want to get the gold,' Anderson accused.

Lamb looked out on the valley, toward the blue mountains on the edge of the San Juan. He was silent for a long time, a dusty, stringy man with a sort of puzzlement in his eyes. He said, 'This gold is sort of used now. It ain't just like brand new stuff, somehow. Even so I guess I'd stay and try to get it back, if I thought there was any chance.'

'What do you mean, it's used?'

'I killed four men because of it. I lost a good buckskin horse.'

'It was our neck or theirs!' Anderson said.

'Sure. I know that.' Lamb frowned. 'I ain't saying gold is bad, you understand, but it can cause you a pile of grief. I take it as an omen that the wind covered this mess of it up.' Lamb rose. He smoothed with his feet the furrows he had made. 'Let's move on.'

'And leave a fortune just a hundred feet away from us?'

184

'It's the longest hundred feet God ever created, Andy.'

'You don't want the gold?' Anderson asked.

'Not that, exactly. If we could get it, I'd take my share of it, but I'm kind of relieved that we can't get it.'

Anderson licked his lips. 'Suppose I get it out by myself?'

'I give my share to you right this minute. Now, let's go. We'll have to hump to get a tight camp set up in the San Juan before winter.' He started down the dune.

'Then it's mine!'

'Sure, it's yours forever, Andy. Come on.'

'You won't come around claiming half of it after I get it out?'

Lamb stopped and swung around. 'You don't mean you're going to try?'

'I'm not going to run away from a fortune.'

'We'll find another one,' Lamb said.

'No! I know where this one is.'

*   *   *

An hour later Anderson was in the same place, sitting with his rifle across his knees. He allowed that an obstacle stood between him and the treasure but the proximity of the gold outweighed all other considerations. He watched the dust where Lamb was riding away. Lamb might be trying to trick him. Lamb could have lied about the number of steps from the cottonwood.

Darkness came down on the great valley that had been a lake in ancient times. Purple shades ran in the hollows of the dunes, and the crests of the ridges looked like the black manes of horses struggling toward the sky. A mighty silence lay on the piles of sand that had been gathering here for eons.

Anderson was still sitting on the sand above the treasure. He rose at last, sticking his rifle barrel down into the dune. When he went across the shallow sand to where his horse was tied in the cottonwoods, the animal stamped and whinnied. It could wait. Anderson found a dead limb. He used it to replace his rifle as a marker. He counted his steps back to the cottonwood. They were a few less than Lamb had said.

That night he camped on Medano Creek, waking a dozen times to listen to small noises. The dunes were huge, taking pale light from the ice points of the stars. At dawn he was riding through the pinons, searching for a less exposed campsite. He found it near a spring in a narrow gulch that looked out on the dunes. From here he could see part of the mouth of Medano Gulch, and he could see the marker he had left on the dune. He built a bough hut near the spring, fretting because it seemed to be taking time from more important work.

That afternoon he killed a deer, standing for several moments after the shot, wondering

186

how far the sound of his rifle had carried; and then he was in a fever to get back to where he could watch the dunes.

There had been wind that morning. The marker was standing above the sand by eighteen inches or more. Anderson experienced a quick leap of hope; the wind had built the dunes, the wind had hidden the gold, and the wind could also uncover it again. It was a great thought.

Before evening the marker was almost covered. At dawn it was gone.

Without eating breakfast Anderson hurried from the trees and paced across the sand, taking sightings. Scrabbling on his hands and knees, he found the limb a few inches below the surface of the dune. He knew that he could always locate the spot but the limb was a tangible mark that gave him more of a link with the treasure than anything he carried in his mind. He set another marker at the base of the dune, a huge rock, three hundred and fifty steps from the cottonwood.

Sitting in his camp that afternoon, he worried about the loss of landmarks. The gray rocks on the mountain might change or slide away, the cottonwood and the dead spruce might blow over. He returned quickly to the broad gulch and set a row of rocks fifty paces apart, burying them on solid ground below the sand, in a line which pointed toward the treasure.

Now he felt better. Rocks were solid and heavy; they would not blow away. Going back to his camp in the evening, a brand new doubt struck him: suppose the wind uncovered his line of rocks. Anyone riding past would wonder why they had been placed so. The extensions of the thought worried Anderson until late in the night. He rose and went down the hill to have a look.

He put his face close to the sand, sighting. The surface was gently rippled. He could not see any stones, not even the large one he had left exposed purposely. He felt that his presence protected the gold; he was loath to leave. For a long time he stood shivering in the night. When he finally started back to his camp, a light wind swept down through the pinons. It was a dawn wind, natural; it came every morning and had nothing to do with the great winds that had built the dunes. But Anderson felt that it was a deliberate betrayal, and so he went back to the edge of the sand and stayed there until the wind died away.

During the days and weeks that passed he grew hollow-eyed and gaunt. He begrudged the time it required to get meat when he was out of food. His rest was never unbroken, disturbed by dreams of a powerful wind that swept the sand away to the rocks, leaving his sacks of gold lying in a long row where anyone could see them. That happened over and over, and then he dreamed of running down the hill to find himself entrapped in waist-deep sand among the trees. He struggled there, while out on the flat men were riding without haste to pick up the sacks. And then he would waken, trembling and almost ill from frustration.

Light snows dusted the valley. Whiteness lay in the grim wrinkles of the *Sangre de Cristo* and the dunes sparkled in the frosty air of early morning; but the snow never lasted long upon the sand. A season of winds followed. They gathered out of the southwest, twisting into crazy patterns when they struck the dunes. Sometimes Anderson saw sand streaming in four directions on ridges that lay close to each other.

When the wind was at its strongest he never heard the singing. The sounds came only with diminishing winds or when the blow was first rising. High-pitched music skirling from the ridges, running clear and sharp, then clashing like sky demons fighting when the wind made sudden changes. Anderson heard the singing at times when he stood at the foot of the dunes in still air, sensing the powerful rush of currents far above.

Sometimes, crouched in the doorway of his hut, he watched the queer half daylight of the storms and read strange words into the music. There was something in the sounds that wailed of lostness and of madness, of the times after centuries of rain had ceased, when the earth was drying and man was unknown.

Each time the wind ceased, while his ears still held music that could never be named or written into notes, Anderson went down the hill to see what changes had been made.

The dunes were never the same and yet they were always the same, soft contours on the slopes, wind-sharpened ridges, hollows that went down to natural earth, white streaks where the heavier particles of sand gathered to themselves. A million tons of sand could shift in a few minutes but nothing was really changed.

The wind did as it pleased; it did not do Anderson's work for him. Sometimes his limb marker was buried twenty feet deep; sometimes he found it lying ten feet lower than it had been. He always put it upright.

Long snows fell upon the valley. Deer came down from the hills. On clear days Anderson saw smoke at distant farms where pioneers were toughing out the winter. He thought of Lamb, snug by now in some tight, red-rocked valley of the San Juan. Lamb probably was searching for gold again, not really caring whether he found it or not. The thought infuriated Anderson.

Anderson was on the dunes one day when a wind, running steadily along the surface of the ground, began to eat into the side of the slope that covered the sacks. Tense and choked-up, he watched it, first with suspicion, and then with hope. Faster than any tool man could ever create, the numberless hands of the wind scooped sand until a rounding cove appeared. Anderson's largest marker rock sat on bare ground now. The cove extended, an oval running deeper and deeper into the side of the dune where his gold lay.

Anderson followed the receding sand as a man would pace after a falling tide. He counted until he knew he was within fifteen steps of the gold. Whirling around the edges of the cove, digging, lifting, the wind took sand away until Anderson knew he stood no farther than ten feet from the first sack. He could not stand inactive any longer. He began to burrow like an animal, and the wind worked with him effortlessly. He shouted incoherently when his hand closed on soft buckskin. The first sack.

It became an evil moment. Somewhere on Mosca or Medano or Music, or perhaps all three, there was a sudden change. The wind now came from a different direction. Sand poured down the slope faster than Anderson could dig. It grew around his legs, covering them. Sand rippled down the surface of the dune. It fell directly from the air. Cursing, half blinded, Anderson dug furiously. He might as well have been scooping water from a lake with his hands.

He was forced back as slowly as he had come. The cove filled up again. He stood in the wide gulch at last, on shallow sand where there never seemed to be appreciable change.

Almost exhausted, he stumbled away, muttering like a man insane. The wind began to lessen and the dunes sang to him, singing him back to his miserable hut of boughs among the pinons. He threw the sack of gold inside and lay by the spring until he was trembling from cold.

That night there was no wind. He crouched over his fire, and his eyes were as red as the flames that blossomed from the pinon sticks. It was no use to wait on the wind, for the wind would only torture him. He must do everything by his own efforts.

*   *   *

The next day he rode to a farm in the valley. The snow lay unevenly where ground had been ploughed, a pitiful patch of accomplishment, considering the vastness, Anderson thought. There was a low log barn, unchinked. A black-bearded young man came to the doorway of a one-room cabin with a rifle in his hands.

'I'm a prospector,' Anderson explained. 'I'm looking for some boards to build me a place. Been living in a bough hut.'

'Build a cabin.' The farmer's dark eyes were watchful, but they were also lonely.

'I lost my packhorse and all my tools coming over Music.'

The man shook his head. 'I've got an axe and a plough—and that's about it. Come spring, my brothers will be back with some things we need—I hope.' He studied the shaggy condition of Anderson's horse. 'Come in and eat.'

The cabin was primitive. A man must be a fool, Anderson thought, to try to make a farm in this valley. The farmer's name was George Linkman. His loneliness came out in talk and he wanted Anderson to stay the night. From him Anderson found out that there was a man about ten miles east who had hauled a load of lumber from New Mexico the fall before and hadn't got around to building with it yet.

Ten miles east. That put the place close to the dunes, somewhere against the mountains.

Anderson rode away with one suspicion cleared from his mind: Linkman was not the man who had followed him and Lamb to the Huerfano. Linkman's voice was much too deep. But who was this man against the hills close to the dunes? Anderson was uneasy when he found the place at the mouth of a small stream, and realized that it was not more than two miles from his own camp.

He was reassured somewhat by the fact that the log buildings were old. There had been more cultivation here than at Linkman's place. No one was at home. He saw the pile of lumber, already warping. He stared at it greedily.

The man came riding in from the valley side of the foothills. He was a stocky, middle-aged man, clean shaved, with gray in his hair. His faded mackinaw was ragged. He greeted Anderson heartily and asked him why he hadn't gone inside to warm up and help himself to food.

'Just got here,' Anderson said. *The voice* . . . No, it wasn't the voice of the man who had come to Mendoza's place. That man had been young.

The farmer's name was Burl Hollister. While he cooked a meal he kept bragging about the potatoes he had grown last summer. There was a hillside cellar still half full of them to prove his boast. Nothing would do but Anderson must stay all night with him.

By candlelight Hollister talked of the new ground he would break next spring, of the settlers who would come to the valley in time. Anderson nodded, watching him narrowly. This place was too close to the dunes, but of course it had been here long before Anderson and Lamb made their terrible mistake in the hollow of the sand.

Anderson brought up the matter of lumber and tools, speaking guardedly of a streak of gold he had discovered on Mosca Pass.

'Tools I can spare,' Hollister said slowly, 'but that lumber—that's something else. I figured to build the old lady a lean-to kitchen with it before she comes back in the spring. I was aiming to surprise her. This place ain't much for a woman yet, but in time—'

'You could get more lumber before spring.' Anderson drew a sack of gold from his shirt. There was not much in the sack, perhaps a pound and a half, for he had left most of it in the buckskin pouch he had recovered from the dunes.

After some hesitation Hollister untied the strings and dipped his fingers into the yellow grains. 'Good Lord!' he breathed. 'Is that all gold?'

'You could buy more lumber, Hollister.'

'Tools, yes,' the farmer murmured. 'I can spare tools, but doggone, it's a long haul to get boards here.' He kept pinching the gold between his thumb and two fingers. 'Is this from your claim on Mosca?'

Anderson did not answer too hastily. 'No, that came from the San Juan. I don't know yet what I have on Mosca.'

'All of it for the lumber?'

Anderson nodded.

Not looking up, Hollister said, 'All right.'

He hauled the lumber and tools the next day to the bottom of the hill below Anderson's camp. Hollister brought also a bushel of potatoes. He spent most of the morning digging and lining a tiny cellar to keep them from freezing. When that was done he said, 'I'll help you carry the boards up here.'

'You've done enough,' Anderson said. 'I've got to level off a place here first.'

'You're welcome to stay with me till spring.'

'Thanks, but I'd rather be closer to my work.'

Hollister nodded, staring across at the dunes. 'Sort of pretty, ain't they?'

'Not to me. There's too much sand,' Anderson said, and then he began to worry about the implications of his statement. He was glad when Hollister left.

Now that he had the lumber, Anderson began to doubt that it would serve his purpose. He had planned to work only at night but desperation was growing in him. In the spring riders would be coming to Medano and Mosca constantly. It was better to take a chance now on Linkman and Hollister, so far the only men who knew he was here.

But he retained caution. Until he knew how the lumber would serve, he would not try to tunnel directly toward the gold. He started a hundred yards away from his line of rocks, in a direction at a right angle to the treasure. He drove short boards into the sand, overhead and on the sides of his projected tunnel. Then he shoveled, framing more lumber to support the board as soon as the sand fell away from them. Sand poured through the cracks and between the warped edges where the boards did not fit tightly. He nailed more lumber over the cracks. In a month of brutal labor he made ten feet. And then one day when he was shoveling back, he heard a cracking sound. He got clear just before the tunnel collapsed.

He was standing with a shovel in his hand, too spent to curse, when Linkman rode up. Anderson did not hear him until the farmer was quite close, but when he saw the long shadow of the horse upon the sand, he dropped his shovel and leaped to grab his rifle.

'Hey!' Linkman cried. 'What's the matter?'

Anderson lowered his rifle, but he kept staring at the visitor, who was looking curiously at the ends of boards sticking from the sand.

'That's a funny place for a potato cellar.' Linkman tried to smile but he was too uneasy to make it real. He fumbled on, 'I thought your mine was up on Mosca.'

Anderson did not say anything. He saw the slow breaking of something in Linkman's expression, a fear, a disturbed sensation that Linkman tried to conceal. The man could not have made himself more clear if he had put a forefinger to his temple and made a circular motion.

'I was just riding around,' Linkman said vaguely. 'I guess I'll be going. I was just scouting for a place to get some firewood.' He rode away.

Anderson went back to his camp. When he knelt at the spring he knew why Linkman had thought him mad. His beard was matted, his eyes hollow and bloodshot, his lips tight against his teeth. He was jolted for a few moments, and then he drank and turned his mind once more to the problem of the treasure.

It struck him suddenly. He would build his tunnel in the open, where he could make the boards tight and the framing strong. He would build sections that would fit together snugly, large enough for a man to crawl through easily. The next time the wind gouged out a hole in the direction of his gold, he would have his sections ready to lay in place. Let the damned wind cover them. The tunnel would be there, even if it was under two hundred feet of sand.

There were omissions in his plan that he did not care to dwell on at the moment; overall, it was a beautiful idea and that was enough. He rose to cook a meal and was annoyed to find he had no meat.

He found the horse tracks when he was hunting deer in the pinons above his camp. He spent the whole afternoon chasing up and down the hills until he knew that someone had been watching him, not only recently but for a long time. Instead of fear, he felt an insane fury that made him grind his teeth.

That night another gale came out of the southwest, coursing toward the high passes. Restless in his cold hut, Anderson heard the howling of it; and later, the singing of the sands when the wind began to decrease.

Clean morning sunlight on the great buff hills showed Anderson that they were unchanged. The ends of the boards from his collapsed tunnel were hidden now, and for the hundredth time his limb marker above the gold was covered. For several moments he was motionless.

There were forces here that he could never conquer, a challenge that would lead him to wreckage. Lamb had known what he was doing when he wasted not a moment, but rode away. For the first time Anderson felt an urge to leave, but he knew that the wind could undo what it had done; and if he went away, he might be haunted forever by the thought that what he had waited for happened one hour, a day, or a week, after he quit.

He went down the hill and began to build the sections of his tunnel lining. He piled them on the shallow sand. He built them so that one man could drag them into place when the time came. It was not heavy work but it tired him more each day. He went at it with desperate urgency, thinking that the wind might choose a time to dig toward his treasure when he was unprepared.

Dizzy spells began to bother him during the three days it took to build the boxes. He had been eating scraps, or very little; and his mind had been burning up the resources of his body. This he realized, but time might run away from him, and so he staggered on at his work, resting only when his vision darkened.

Utterly spent, he finished the boxes one

afternoon when there was no wind. He slumped down behind a pile of them, letting his hands fall limply into the fine sand.

Sleep struck him like a maul. He dreamed of the running fight across Medano, of the easy life on the Huerfano. He trembled in his sleep, a young man who was old and gaunt. A voice roused him slowly.

'Anderson! Anderson! Where are you?'

Groggily, Anderson tried to come out of his exhaustion. He thought he was back on the floor of Mendoza's house, with his feet swollen and scratched. The last pursuer had come across the pass and was inquiring about him and the mule.

'Hey, Anderson! Don't tell me you've got lost in one of those sluice boxes.'

Anderson stared at his boots. There was no doubt of it: the voice was that of the man who had survived the chase, the same cool voice of a young man who would not give up. Anderson's rifle was in one of the boxes. He could not remember which one.

His muscles dragged wearily when he rose. He could not believe the man sitting there on the horse was Hollister.

'Sleeping in the middle of daylight!' Hollister grinned. His clean shaved face was bright. His gray hair showed below the frayed edges of his scotch cap. He frowned at the boxes. 'You're a long ways from water with those sluices, Anderson.'

Hollister was the man. Now that Anderson could separate his voice from his appearance, he was able to get rid of the inaccurate picture he had built of Hollister. Anderson moved around the boxes until he found his rifle. He remembered the flight across Medano long ago. It was Hollister's fault and his fault that the gold was here.

Hollister said, 'You've worked yourself plumb string-haltered, Ander—' He stopped, staring into the muzzle of Anderson's rifle. 'What's the matter?'

'You're the man that followed me and Lamb to the Huerfano! You're no farmer. You've been watching me ever since I've been here.'

Hollister kept his hands on the saddle horn. He looked at Anderson gravely. 'The farm belongs to a man who wanted to go back to Kansas for the winter. I'm the man, all right. Now there's just two of us. The wind got your gold, didn't it, Anderson?'

Anderson stepped away from the boxes, edging to the side so that if Hollister made his horse rear the act would not interfere with the shot. Anderson was ready to kill the man. He wanted to. All he lacked was some small puff of provocation.

Hollister gave him none. He sat quietly, moving only his head. 'When I came back over the pass, I found the panniers and the packsaddle you threw away. There was only one place where you two could have covered your tracks that day—here. I knew you'd come back.

'There's two of us, Anderson. You're as well off as you were before. I'm much better off, thanks to your partner.' He gave the thought time to grow. 'You left the gold here. The wind covered it. Your partner should have known better, but of course we were pushing you hard and you didn't have much choice. There's ways to get at it, Anderson. How deep is it?'

Anderson did not answer. He still wanted to kill Hollister but he knew he could not do it.

'The two of us can get it out of there,' Hollister said. 'I know a way.' He looked at the boxes. 'That won't work. You figure to make a tunnel of them, don't you? The sand will blow in one end and pour into the other. I know a better way, Anderson.'

He was bargaining only because the rifle was on him, Anderson thought. But no, Hollister must not be sure of where the treasure lay.

'I've got every ounce of every sack you dropped on Medano,' Hollister said. 'That goes in the split too. You know where the rest is. I'm not sure. You can't get it out. I know a way. I could have killed you, Anderson, months ago. If I had been sure of where the sacks were, maybe I would have.' He smiled. 'That's all in the past now. There's gold enough for ten men.'

Anderson grounded his rifle. 'You know a

way to get it out?'

'Yes.'

That was the bait, Anderson thought, the bait that would bring the deadfall crashing down on his neck. But belief began to grow in him. The thought that he could trust Hollister became more important than any idea the man had about recovering the treasure.

'Think about it,' Hollister said. 'You've no one to ask about me. I'm an odd man inside. When I give my word, Anderson, before God, it's good.' He turned his horse and rode away. The faded mackinaw covering his broad back was an easy target all the way to the cotton-woods.

Anderson had believed him while he was here, but now the worms of suspicion began to twist and turn again. For a week Anderson did not go down upon the sands. He stayed in camp or hunted, and he saw no more fresh horse tracks on the hills. The winds came, piling sand in a long, curving ramp against his boxes, and the wind uncovered the boards where he had experimented with a tunnel. There was something ancient and ghostly in the look of the lumber sticking from the dune.

He knew with a dreary certainty that men could not defy the work of a million years of wind. The caprice of the gales would expose the treasure when the time came, but that might be a century from now.

There was also the thought that it could be

tomorrow, and that was what held Anderson, gnawed with the fear of defeat only, no longer dreaming of what gold could buy. It struck him that if he could transfer the burden of worry, which in a way was exactly what Lamb had done, then he might be free.

He rode to see Hollister.

The man was sitting by a warm fire, smoking his pipe. 'Out of potatoes, Anderson? The darned things are beginning to sprout. It must be getting near spring.'

Near spring. Months of Anderson's life had flowed into the sands. He had lived like a brute.

'You look some better,' Hollister said. He spoke like a neighbor being pleasant but knowing that there was bargaining to come.

'This way of yours to move the sand . . .' Anderson let it trail off. There was no way to move the sand. His own ideas had been sure and clear about that once, but now he knew better.

'Yeah?' Hollister's eyes tightened.

'You've got the sacks I threw away on Medano?'

Hollister nodded.

'For them I'll tell you where the rest is, and you can have it all—if you can dig it out.'

Hollister cocked his head. 'I'd rather have you working with me—for half of everything.'

'You're afraid I won't tell the truth? I thought Lamb had lied to me too, Hollister.

He didn't. He paced the distance. I recovered one sack of gold, right where it was supposed to be.'

Hollister rubbed his lips together slowly.

'One sack is all. The wind will break your heart, Hollister.'

'I can beat it.'

'Give me what I left behind on the pass. The rest is yours.'

Hollister's eyes were bright. 'Let's go up and take a look at the dunes.'

The hooves of the horses made soft sounds in the broad gulch. The full weight of the hills bore on Anderson and he wondered how he had ever been fool enough to think he could outwit the dunes. He knew better now and he had learned before his mind broke on the problem.

'They're yours, Hollister.'

The older man's satisfied expression threw a jet of worry into Anderson. Maybe he was selling out too cheaply. It was an effort to stick with his decision.

Hollister said. 'Your sacks are buried just inside the door of the potato cellar.'

Anderson pointed to the limb on the dune. He told Hollister about the rocks under the sand and the sighting marks and the number of steps from the tree.

'I knew most of that from watching you,' Hollister said, 'but I wasn't sure. Why'd you start the tunnel over there?' His gaze was sharp and hard.

'I did that after I knew you were spying.'

Hollister knew the truth when he heard it. 'It would have saved me gold if I had killed you, wouldn't it?' In the same conversational tone he went on, 'I'm going to bring a ditch down from Medano. I'll flume it through the sand and let the water wash away what I want moved.'

Water would seep into the sand. It would run out of cracks in the flume, causing the sections to buckle. The eternal wind would work easily while Hollister was floundering and cursing his broken plan. Anderson had never felt sorry for himself. Now he had sympathy for Hollister.

'Don't come back,' Hollister said. 'We've made our bargain. I'll kill you if you hang around or come back.'

Anderson went up the hill to his camp. The first signs of spring were breaking on the edges of the valley. He hadn't noticed them before. He stared for a while at the bough hut. It was a hovel unworthy of a Digger Indian. *I stayed in that all winter.*

He took his camping gear and kicked the hut apart.

Out on the sand, Hollister was walking slowly. He had found the line of rocks. He turned and sighted, and then he looked at the boards where the wrecked tunnel had been. There would always be in his mind, Anderson knew, doubt that Anderson had told the truth. The sand would defy him, the winds would mock him, and the singing on the ridges would jeer him.

When Anderson rode away, he saw Hollister dragging the boxes with his horse, dragging them up to where he would build a flume that would break his heart. The struggle of the horse and man against the sand was a picture that Anderson would never forget.

He found the sacks in the potato cellar where Hollister had said. He opened each one and ran his hand inside and afterward looked at the grains of gold clinging to his cracked and roughened skin. The sand had done that too.

He stuffed the sacks inside his shirt. At once the weight was intolerable. Perhaps somewhere out on the floor of the valley where there was no sand to blow over it . . . No, gold was not to be buried. He would put it inside the pack on his horse. Half of it was Lamb's.

Anderson hesitated and then he dropped one bag on the floor. He thought it was a small enough price to pay for transferring a crushing burden. He rode away, going toward the purple mountains of the San Juan Basin. For a while the tug of the treasure of the dunes was still strong, but he kept going until at last he knew beyond doubt that he had made a good decision.

At sunset he turned to look back. Against the high range the buff hills were small, pale, beautiful, changeless. Anderson raised his eyes to the crimson glory flaming on the summits of the Blood of Christ Mountains, watching quietly until the color seeped away; and then he rode on, knowing that tonight he would sleep as he had not slept for months.

* * *

The winds still sing across the dark manes of the sand dunes, wailing, if the ear can understand, of the man who lived for thirty years in a little hut among the pinons. He dressed in cast-off garments that ranchers brought him. He raised dogs that ran wild, eating them when times were lean. He was crazy as a bedbug, for he talked of gold he was going to wash from the sands. The wind alternately covered and uncovered the rotting sections of a flume he had tried to build around the shoulder of the dune.

He said that the wind knew a great secret and that four times the wind had almost showed him the secret; and then in the next breath he would curse the wind with such insane vehemence that people were glad to get away from him. There was something vicious about the old man, but there also was something pitiful and lost in the record of his life.

On a bright fall day when the aspens on Medano were golden streaks against the mountains he died on the sand with a shovel in his hands. George Linkman, a pioneer rancher, found him there with the hungry dogs whining and edging closer to him. Linkman shot the dogs. One yellow cur went howling across the sand almost to the rotting trunk of a huge, fallen cottonwood before it died.

There had been a strong wind the night before. When Linkman carried the old man toward the trees to bury him, he saw a line of rocks, a solid line of them, running from where the dead dog lay to the base of the first dune. It appeared that the crazy old devil had tried at one time to build a dam to catch the floodwaters of Medano Creek in the spring.

The next time Linkman came by the dunes—he was an old man and his riding days were numbered—he observed that the wind had covered the rocks once more.